Him She Loves?

A CHARLOTTE ZOLOTOW BOOK
CZ

Books by M. E. Kerr

DINKY HOCKER SHOOTS SMACK!
Best of the Best Books (YA) 1970–83 (ALA)
Best Children's Books of 1972, *School Library Journal*
ALA Notable Children's Books of 1972

IF I LOVE YOU, AM I TRAPPED FOREVER?
Honor Book, *Book World* Children's Spring Book Festival,
    1973
Outstanding Children's Books of 1973, *The New York Times*

THE SON OF SOMEONE FAMOUS
(AN URSULA NORDSTROM BOOK)
Best Children's Books of 1974, *School Library Journal*
"Best of the Best" Children's Books, 1966–1978,
    School Library Journal

IS THAT YOU, MISS BLUE?
(AN URSULA NORDSTROM BOOK)
Outstanding Children's Books of 1975, *The New York Times*
ALA Notable Children's Books of 1975
Best Books for Young Adults, 1975 (ALA)

LOVE IS A MISSING PERSON
(AN URSULA NORDSTROM BOOK)

I'LL LOVE YOU WHEN YOU'RE MORE LIKE ME
(AN URSULA NORDSTROM BOOK)
Best Children's Books of 1977, *School Library Journal*

GENTLEHANDS
(An Ursula Nordstrom Book)
Best Books for Young Adults, 1978 (ALA)
ALA Notable Children's Books of 1978
Best Children's Books of 1978, *School Library Journal*
Winner, 1978 Christopher Award
Best Children's Books of 1978, *The New York Times*

LITTLE LITTLE
ALA Notable Children's Books of 1981
Best Books for Young Adults, 1981 (ALA)
Best Children's Books of 1981, *School Library Journal*
Winner, 1981 Golden Kite Award,
   Society of Children's Book Writers

WHAT I REALLY THINK OF YOU
(A Charlotte Zolotow Book)
Best Children's Books of 1982, *School Library Journal*

ME ME ME ME ME: Not a Novel
(A Charlotte Zolotow Book)
Best Books for Young Adults, 1983 (ALA)

M.E. KERR

Him She Loves?

1 8 🔥 1 7

——————— HARPER & ROW, PUBLISHERS ———————

Cambridge, Philadelphia, San Francisco, London, Mexico City, São Paulo, Sydney

——————— NEW YORK ———————

3250

Library of Congress Cataloging in Publication Data
Kerr, M. E.
  Him she loves?

  "A Charlotte Zolotow book"—Half t.p.
  SUMMARY: When seventeen-year-old Henry Schiller fell
in love with Valerie Kissenwiser, he never suspected
that their romance would become national television's
funniest comedy routine.
  I. Title.
PZ7.K46825Hi 1984   [Fic]   83-48818
ISBN 0-06-023238-2
ISBN 0-06-023239-0 (lib. bdg.)

To Lorelei Lewis
Hi, Lolly!

1

Soon I would be laughed at on national television, and so in love I couldn't chew my food, but start at the beginning, when I was just seventeen, and the new kid in town.

Start with the day I first set eyes on her, that bitter cold December afternoon of New Year's Eve.

The oompah band was rehearsing *"Schnitzelbank"* up on the bandstand. My brothers, Ernie and Fred, were in the kitchen cooking up sauerbraten and Königsberger klops. I was sitting at a table in the empty dining room rubbing water spots off silverware.

We were three hours from the grand opening of our restaurant when she flounced through the front door, with snow melting on long black hair that fell past her shoulders, and a face that would change my life.

"Henry?" one of the musicians called out to me, nodding his head in her direction, but I was already on my feet, on my way over to her.

She had her gloves off and had taken one of the menus from the stack on the counter.

"Can I help you?" I asked her. *May, may, may* I help you, I heard my mother's voice in my mind.

"Oh, migosh, I've made a mistake," she said, looking up from the menu.

"What do you mean you've made a mistake?"

"I mean I've made a mistake. Are you Peter?" she said, and then answered the question herself. "No, you're not Peter. You're too young to be Peter."

Peter's was the name of our place.

"I'm Henry," I said. "May I help you?"

"I doubt it a lot."

"What's the problem?"

"It never occurred to me Peter's would be German."

"What did you think Peter's would be?"

"Not German," she said. "I want to make a Sweet Sixteen party."

"We have room in the back for parties," I said. "We can seat forty, unless it's for tonight. We're pretty well booked tonight."

2

"It's not for tonight, but we can't have it here, anyway."

"If you don't like German food," I said, "we can do fish. We can do lobster, we can do prime ribs of beef, frogs' legs—"

She made a face.

"I'm just suggesting," I said. "If frogs' legs turn you off, we can do goulash or goose or—"

She cut me off. "I *like* German food," she said. "I'd almost kill for good strudel, but that's not the point. Do you know what a Sweet Sixteen party is?"

She smelled like summer flowers.

"Is it like a birthday party?"

"It's like a birthday party."

"Is it for you?"

"No," she said in this bored tone. "I think Sweet Sixteen parties are passé, and I'm almost eighteen."

"No one would ever guess it," I said. "You've aged very well."

"Ha! Ha! Look," she said, putting down the menu, "I've made a mistake, that's all. Okay?" She fixed me with her great green eyes and my blood jumped.

"Okay." I shrugged. "But I don't understand what you mean by a mistake. We make the best strudel you'll ever eat."

"You want an explanation?"

"I'd appreciate an explanation."

"My grandmother would kill me is the explanation.

She's making the party for my sister, and if she heard I'd picked a German restaurant she'd go through the roof."

I still didn't get it.

"Why would she go through the roof?"

The oompah band started up, and Otto, its leader, bellowed out, *"Ist das nicht ein Schnitzelbank?"*

"We're Jewish," she said. "My grandmother doesn't buy Volkswagens or Mercedes . . ."

She gave up trying to shout over Otto and the band.

"Ja, das ist ein Schnitzelbank!" Otto sang.

"Hey, Otto!" I yelled over my shoulder. "I can't hear the young lady!"

Otto piped down.

"You *did* hear the young lady, though?" she asked me.

"Yes," I said, "but we're not real Germans. I mean, I've never even been to Germany."

"This place is real German, though. You know?"

She was about to reach for her gloves.

I said, "My name is Henry Schiller. Uh. I just moved to Seaville."

"Well, I'm sorry, Henry. Nothing personal." She looked right into my eyes again and made me ache.

"I'm starting Seaville High on Monday," I said.

"Then I'll probably see you around."

"I didn't get your name."

"I didn't give it to you."

She gave me a slanted smile and said, "I'm Valerie Kissenwiser."

"How do you do."

"How do you do."

"Uh. I hope you find another place for your party."

"Uh," she imitated me, "I don't think we'll have much trouble. Restaurants are the only industry here."

"Yes," I said, "there's a lot of them. . . . Does that mean you can never come here?"

"Does what mean I can never come here?"

"What you said. Uh. About being Jewish."

"Uh"—she was doing it again, that same playful smile tipping her lips—"no, it doesn't mean I can never come here. It just means we're not going to have my sister's Sweet Sixteen party here. Okay?"

"Okay," I said. No more uhs if I could help it. "I'm starting school Monday."

"So you said," she said. "Well. See you."

"See you."

She was forgetting her gloves and I was letting her forget them.

Kissenwiser. I was saying the name over and over to myself. Valerie Kissenwiser.

I rushed ahead of her to hold open the door.

She went through it saying, "Gawd, would Gran have died if I hadn't checked out this place first."

"Yeah, well, give her my love," I said.

"Happy New Year, Henry," she said, and a gust of snow blew in at me.

"Happy New Year!" I called after her, and I stood there in the cold, shivering, teeth chattering, while I watched her run toward a sleek, new, white Riviera convertible.

I took the cashmere gloves back to the kitchen with me.

"Have you set the tables yet?" my brother Ernie asked me.

"I will," I said. "I want to look up something."

"Look up something?"

"In the phone book," I said. I decided not to tell him we'd just lost a Sweet Sixteen party. He was sprinkling salt and caraway seed on leaves of cabbage, and my brother Fred was chopping parsley. There was no sense telling them we'd lost a party before we were even open.

"What have you got to look up in the phone book when the tables aren't set yet?" Ernie wanted to know.

"A girl's number," I said. "I'll set the tables. Don't sweat it."

"You've already met a girl?" Ernie said.

"Please, God, don't let him have already met a girl," Fred said.

"This girl just stopped by to find out when we're opening, and she left her gloves," I said.

"Did she make a reservation?" Ernie said.

"Not yet," I said.

"Please, God, not another Lena in our lives when we're just opening," Fred said.

"She's nothing like Lena," I said.

"If she just stopped by, she's not going to be home yet," Ernie said, "so set the tables and call her later."

"Better still, let one of us call her," Fred said. "All you need is a new romance. All we need is you mixed up with another Lena."

"She's not another Lena," I said. "Pull-lease! Give me a break. I just want to jot down the number."

There was only one Kissenwiser in the Seaville phone book.

I wrote down the number, and the address, then glanced up at my reflection in the mirror.

Before she'd come through the door, I'd been tasting everything from potato dumplings to schnitzel. I checked my smile to see if anything was caught in my teeth. Had I grinned at her with sauerkraut wedged between my incisors? I checked out okay.

I was a big guy—all Schillers were over six feet and blond. I'd been told I resembled the old movie star James Dean, only I had brown eyes and jug ears. If Schillers didn't watch it, we turned into lards. At twenty-eight, my brother Ernie was heading in that direction. At twenty-four, my brother Fred was running six miles a day, in any weather, to keep from it. I was the baby of the family, so far holding my own, thanks to a lot of baseball and football back at

Yorkville High in New York City, before we moved to the tip of Long Island.

"When you finish making love to the mirror," Ernie said, "remember that the tables have to be set."

I went back out to *"Ist das nicht ein Kurz und Lang? Ja, das ist ein Kurz und Lang!"* and grabbed the silverware.

By five-thirty I had the tables set, and one hour to kill before I had to be back in the restaurant. Ernie and my mother lived on the floor above. Fred and his wife rented in Seaville township. I waited until I heard Ernie go upstairs to shower and shave, and Fred leave in his car.

I put on my heavy overcoat and went into the kitchen, where I wrapped a strudel with Reynolds aluminum. I carried it out the back door and put it on the front seat of Peter's Jeep Wagoneer, with the cashmere gloves.

There was a public phone booth in front of Peter's, where I knew no one could listen in. Inside, I shook the snow off my head and deposited a dime.

"Val is napping," a woman's voice said. "She's got a big night ahead of her, so she's not to be disturbed."

"I just want to drop her gloves off," I said. "She left them somewhere, and I have something else for her."

"Who is this?"

"This is Henry Schiller," I said. "Who is this?"

"This is Valerie's grandmother."

"Fine," I said. "I'll just be by with her gloves and something else. I'll just drop them off."

"Henry *who?*" she said.

"That's all right," I said, "you don't know me yet."

"I don't know you yet?"

"I see that you live on Ocean Road," I said. "I'll just ring the bell and slip them through the door."

"Val will be awake by six-thirty," she said.

"Mrs. Kissenwiser? Can . . . *may* I just drop something by? I have an appointment later."

"What can I tell you you want to hear?" she said. "And I'm Mrs. Trump, please."

On the way to Ocean Road, with the help of a road map, through a blinding snowstorm, I began my journey to the heart of Valerie Kissenwiser.

Hoo-ha! as Mrs. Trump, please, would say. . . . Hoo-ha!

2

Everybody in the place was wearing red Tyrolean hats with green feathers we'd placed by their dinner plates. We'd rung in the new year with confetti and balloons, while Otto sang "Auld Lang Syne."

It was about twelve-thirty, and my mother was singing *"Du, Du, Liegst Mir im Herzen"* in a long white gown, carrying a glass of champagne from table to table. She was trying to look intriguing and twenty years younger. She was pretending to be thrilled by some guy who held a cigarette holder between his fingers and blew smoke rings at her, as though that was sexy and mysterious.

I was at the bar, talking with my brother Fred. We

were wearing our dark-green Peter's blazers, with gray flannel pants, white shirts, dark-green ties, and white carnations in our buttonholes.

Fred had the television turned low. He was flipping around the channels, trying to get something live from New York City. The band was on a break, in their green lederhosen, red knee socks, white lace shirts, and red suspenders. As Otto passed me, I told him to go easy on *"Schnitzelbank."*

"This crowd doesn't want to play games tonight," I told him. "New Year's Eve isn't a time for '*Schnitzelbank.*'"

What crowd? We were only half full because of the afternoon's snowstorm. We were drowning in no-shows and stiffs. Stiffs were people who didn't tip the waiter. One party had actually left a card facedown on the table, where a five-dollar bill should have been. When I picked it up, I read: "Thank you for your service but I am morally opposed to the paying of gratuities."

I should have been morally opposed to taking back the bratwurst with raisins and apples the lady decided she didn't want, after she saw everyone else's brisket of beef with horseradish sauce.

"We never should have left New York," Fred said. I was thinking that, too.

"We only did forty dinners," Fred said.

"Well, we're new," I said. "And the weather."

On the TV screen Times Square was mobbed.

11

"That's where we should be," Fred said.

A year ago I'd been part of the crowd, dragging Lena Bunch with me, first time in a tux, her first time in a long dress. No matter how long I live, she shouted at me, I'll always remember this night and these lilies you gave me, and being in love when the ball fell from the Times Square tower!

Fred pushed the remote control and came up with something from Atlantic City.

"In a moment," the announcer was saying, "we'll be bringing you Al Kiss live from the elegant Blackjack Café, so stay tuned for Al Kiss live!"

"That's more than his jokes are," Fred said. "I saw him out in Las Vegas on my honeymoon and he was doing bits Alan King did ten years ago."

I noticed that the violinist accompanying my mother was swirling around after her in the other room with his fly open.

"Oh, great!" I said.

"What?" Fred said.

"Nothing," I said, and someone put a cigarette to a string of balloons: POP POP POP POP. "Hap-py New Year!" someone else shouted, and then they came through the front door.

Four of them, two couples, and she was half of one of the couples.

I walked across to them and did a little bow.

"Happy New Year," I said. "Would you like a table?"

12

"We don't have room in the car," she said.

She had her long black hair pulled back, and large gold loop earrings on.

"We'll just have a drink at the bar," her date said. He said to the other fellow, "Shall we just have a drink at the bar, Roy?"

They were both wearing Burberrys trench coats, and the girls were in polo coats, dresses, and high-heeled boots.

"Let's have a drink at the bar," her date said.

"Why don't you and Roy have one at the bar?" she said a little mockingly behind him, and rolled her green eyes to the ceiling.

"That's what I thought," her date said. But she wasn't really making fun of him. It was her tease. She teased. He wasn't the type you made fun of. He was the type you cast in toothpaste commercials, or voted most handsome, or lost your steady girl to.

He was Mr. Wonderful, and my gut ached.

The band was back, playing "Lilli Marlene," and my mother was going upstairs for a break.

Good.

My mother crimped my style even more than a Mr. Wonderful.

How could you come across cool and sly in front of someone who was always yelling at you to put the toilet seat down before leaving the bathroom?

"Do you want to keep your coat?" I asked Valerie Kissenwiser.

"Why don't you keep it?" she said. "It likes diamonds and penthouses and all the things kept coats like."

The other girl hooted, and the boys walked up to the bar, where Fred asked them if they were nineteen.

They were reaching for their wallets. Even if they weren't nineteen they'd have identification that said they were.

"Uh. Thanks for the strudel," Valerie said.

"Uh. You're welcome."

"Henry, this is my sister, Jody. Jody, this is the one who brought the strudel by this afternoon."

"When are you going to be sixteen?" I asked her. She had braces on her teeth and the promise of turning into her sister in a few years.

"How did you know I'm going to be sixteen?" she said. "Val, how did he know I'm going to be sixteen?"

"Hey!" the boy named Roy called from the bar. "They've got it on TV."

I didn't have to tell Jody Kissenwiser how I knew she was going to be sixteen. The girls ran to the bar.

I walked when I wanted to fly. I stood behind them while Fred fixed ginger ale for Jody, scotch and soda for the boys ("Johnnie Walker Black Label!" Valerie's date commanded. "And let me see the bottle!"), and a Perrier with a twist of lemon for Valerie.

"He's not on yet," her date said.

She swung around on her stool, still in her coat, and her knees hit my legs. She said, "My grandmother said you said someday she'd meet you."

"What I said was she hadn't met me yet."

"She thought you said you had plans to meet her."

"What I said was she hadn't met me yet."

Another slanted smile, and that same smell of summer flowers.

Jody Kissenwiser swung around and kneed me the same as her sister had. "How did you know I'm about to be sixteen?"

"Because you look like a Capricorn," I said.

"I'm Aquarius," she said. "I'm the water carrier, not the goat."

"I think he's coming on TV!" Valerie's date said.

"Is he your boyfriend?" I asked Valerie.

"What if he is?" she said. "How could that possibly interest you?"

"Be nice, Val," her sister said. "He brought you your gloves and a strudel in a snowstorm!"

"Okay, he's on!" the boy named Roy shouted. "Val? Jody? . . . Turn it up!" he told Fred.

I'd seen Al Kiss before. Who hadn't? He was in a few movies, comedies about gamblers or gangsters. He was always on TV talk shows doing his routines, and he was often the guest star on afternoon game shows. But mostly he was in nightclubs where only people who liked staying up until two in the morning saw him. He was a stand-up comedian who'd be halfway handsome if he wasn't always making faces or doing takes. He was probably pushing fifty, a little

15

overweight and getting bald.

"Is he a favorite of yours?" Fred asked everyone and didn't get an answer, which was the story of Fred's life. Food answered Fred, people didn't. He could take potatoes and flour and nutmeg and milk and make the lightest dumplings in the world, and he could do things to spareribs people'd pay fifteen dollars to taste. He could turn little pieces of veal into almond-coated medaillons chefs would ask the recipe for, and he could make a head of cabbage into a main dish. And then he could go from the kitchen to the bar, and work another eight hours never off his feet, because Fred was like my father when he was alive: Cooking mellowed him out. They both relaxed by cooking, and in the old days people came to Yorkville in limousines to have dinner at the original Peter's.

"Hey, waiter"—Al Kiss was on—"I want to make a complaint about this chicken you just served me. One leg is shorter than the other. . . . The waiter looks at the guy, and he looks down at the chicken, and then the waiter says to the guy, Are you eating the chicken or dancing with it?"

"Ha! Ha! Ha!" from Valerie's date, then Roy, then Jody, but Valerie was covering her eyes with her hand.

While Al Kiss began another story, I leaned into Valerie and whispered, "Do you want to dance?"

"To that shmaltz?"

16

The band was playing *"Auf Wiedersehen."*

"Take your choice," I said. "Dance to it or listen to it on TV."

"Oh?" she said.

"If you really want to laugh," I said, "watch me try to dance." I was belittling myself with the idea there was something charming about it, particularly if she'd dance with me—because I was a good dancer.

My brother Ernie had taught me to dance. Ernie was my romantic brother. He'd taught me to dance, and to light two cigarettes and hand one to a girl (never mind that I hated to be with girls who smoked), and he taught me this great line to write a girl after I'd once kissed her: *I still feel your breath on my cheek.*

Valerie said, "So you think you're funny, hah? As funny as him?" She nodded in the direction of Al Kiss.

"Easily," I said. "And with my hands tied behind my back."

"Hey, Jody," Valerie said.

"Shhhhh!" Jody said.

Al Kiss said, "And we all know what a Bar Mitzvah is, right? It's a Jewish dude ranch!"

Ha! Ha! Ha! from all of them except Valerie.

"Hey, Jody?" she shouted at her sister again.

"What do you *want*, Val?"

"He thinks he's as funny as Daddy."

"Who thinks he's as funny as Daddy?" Jody said.

"This one," Valerie said. "This Schiller fellow, this Henry Schiller here."

That happened seconds before the phone call.

I was still letting it sink in, letting the blood rush to my face and my ears, when my brother Ernie came up behind me and said there was a personal call for me in the kitchen.

"What are you doing, Henry?" a familiar voice asked. "Are you thinking of me?"

"Lena," I said. I waited to see if my stomach would turn over. It didn't. "Lena?" I said.

"I had to call you because I was thinking of last year when the ball fell and we were together."

"I was thinking that, too," I told her. "Just a while ago."

"Oh, Henry."

"I gave you lilies," I said, "and you said you'd always remember it."

"Not lilies. Little gardenias."

"I knew it was some flower like that."

"And you wrote on the card: 'I still feel your breath on my cheek,' and I almost died when I read that."

"Yeah," I said.

"Oh, Henry. What were you doing before I called?"

"I can't believe what just happened to me," I said. "There's this girl out here named Valerie Kissenwiser. She came in this afternoon and we got to talking and then she came back tonight." I blurted out the entire story to Lena, not about taking the strudel

18

and her gloves to her through a snowstorm, but all the rest, ending with, ". . . and, Lena? It turns out that her father is Al Kiss! I was making fun of him, and it's her father!"

There was a long pause.

Finally she said, "I'm glad I called, Henry. Do you know why?"

"To wish me Happy New Year," I said.

"No, why I'm glad I called."

"Why are you glad you called?"

"I'm glad I called because now I know for once and for all it's over."

"Well, it was over at Christmas," I said.

One hundred and sixty-five dollars for a ring she tossed out the window of a taxi. That's over.

"No, Henry," she said, "now it really is."

For a minute I remembered how she always put her hand on the back of my neck when we kissed, and let one of her fingers trail along my hairline.

"Lena?" I said. "Are you still there?"

She was still there. For a minute I remembered how soft and silky her blond hair always was.

"Are you still there, Lena?" I said, and my stomach was turning over, finally, in a sick surrender.

"I am and I'm not," she said.

This is like mildew, I thought, and my palms were wet. This is never going to go away even after it's gone.

"I'm going to hang up now," she said.

I waited.

"Henry?"

"What?"

"I'm going to hang up now."

"If that's what you want to do."

"It's what I want to do. . . . I just thought you might be thinking about last year at this time."

"I was."

"You were busy with some comedian's daughter."

Another long pause.

"I'm hanging up, Henry."

"Then hang up. I saved up to buy that ring you threw out!"

"I'm hanging up. I don't want to fight."

"Hang up!" I said. "You were the one that wanted a ring so bad and you tossed it out the taxi window!"

"Good-bye," she said.

"You keep saying you're hanging up but you're not hanging up," I said.

"Good-bye forever, Henry. Don't ever call me again."

"Who called who?" I said. "*I* didn't call *you.*"

That got to her.

She hung up.

I wiped some flour off the receiver of the telephone before I put it back on the hook. Ernie was the sloppy cook of my brothers. Ernie'd even manage to get flour in his bed nights.

My heart was banging, and I was gasping for breath,

20

but I charged back out to the bar, ready to get on with my life . . . ready for more of Valerie Kissenwiser.

She was gone.

"They were nice tippers," Fred said.

My mother was singing "What Are You Doing the Rest of Your Life?" to a practically empty room.

3

Monday morning Ernie drove me to school and told me he knew it was tough starting junior year, in a new school, in January, but to remember what Dad always said.

"What did Dad always say?"

Dad never said much to me but things like wash the spinach thoroughly, Henry, and scald it in hot water . . . or cut the meat into small cubes, then slice off the tops of the peppers, discard cores and seeds, and cut the flesh into small pieces.

"Dad always said a turtle never gets anyplace unless he sticks his neck out," Ernie said.

"Good old original Dad," I said. "Have you got a

pencil? I want to write that down."

"Don't be so cynical," Ernie said. "Dad was a good man."

"Now he's a saint," I said. "Saint Peter? Meet Saint Peter."

Since my dad's death he'd become the next thing to a saint in the eyes of my brothers and mother. Everybody but me had forgotten what it was like to compete with the pots and pans for his attention.

My dad was shot to death, refusing to hand over the cash in our register to some thug, who was back out on the streets before we sold our place in York-ville.

I don't think I ever forgave my dad for that.

In my family's eyes he was some kind of a hero, but I'd rather he'd lost the four hundred thirty-five dollars, and hung around so I could have gotten to know him.

I was twelve when we all piled into the limo with its lights on at noon, and drove him out to some overcrowded cemetery in Brooklyn. I was in the backseat trying to remember if we'd ever had a con-versation anywhere but in a kitchen, on any subject besides one like how to stuff ham horns, or roll cab-bage leaves.

I thanked Ernie for the ride, and began my first day at Seaville High.

Of course, I was looking around for her.

I thought I caught a glimpse of her long black hair,

ahead of me in the crowd, in between classes, mid-morning.

I couldn't find her anywhere in the cafeteria at noon. I sat by myself eating something called chili chow. It was a combination of chili and chow mein that our dog, who'd eat Brillo if you put it in his bowl, wouldn't eat.

Then I looked out at the parking lot behind school, to see if I could spot the white Riviera convertible. There was no sign of it. I ambled back to my locker to get my books for afternoon classes, feeling wimpy and homesick for Yorkville High.

After a class called Health and Human Behavior, I all but forgot her. What made me forget her was what happened to me in that class. It was taught by a big red-necked, red-faced teacher named Mr. Peddle, whose nickname was Piddle. He was just an inch away from the edge. You wouldn't be surprised to see him froth at the mouth.

Everyone in the class was assigned an identity that posed a typical teenage problem. There was an alcoholic, a drug addict, someone supposed to be suicidal, a gay, etc. Piddle said since we were a generation that seemed insistent on equal rights for males and females, the class assignments wouldn't be concerned with male/female roles.

A minute after the class began, he called out my name.

24

"Come forward, Mr. Schiller," he said when I raised my hand.

Then when I got to the front of the room, Piddle began circling me like a curious scientist inspecting an extraterrestrial.

"Mr. Schiller," he began, "you are at somewhat of a disadvantage arriving late in the semester."

"Yes, sir."

His hands were on his hips, jacket open, tie stained from whatever it had dropped in during lunch, zipper of his pants not fastened all the way up, leather shoes practically crying through their tongues: Polish us, polish us, polish us.

"However," he continued, "we lost a member of this class when she moved to California, and you may take over her assignment."

"Yes, sir."

"She was in the fifth month of her pregnancy, Mr. Schiller."

"Sir?"

"I *said* she was in the fifth month of her pregnancy. Her class identity was an unmarried, pregnant teen-ager."

I had nothing to say to that, and I noticed that no one in the class dared laugh. That told me a lot about Piddle.

"You are in the second trimester of your pregnancy, Mr. Schiller, too late for an abortion."

"Yes, sir."

"Since you opted to have your baby, you'd better do your homework on carrying it, the delivery, and your plans afterward."

"Yes, sir."

"I'll be calling on you to find out how you're progressing, Mr. Schiller," he ended this little interview with me. "Be prepared."

After that class, I made my first friend in Seaville High. He was fat, not chubby or a little overweight, but gross. He followed me as I went out the door, and told me his name was Nelson Flower.

"Piddle's a sadist," he said, "and he's crazy besides."

"I figured he'd stepped off the curb."

"He saves his most crazy self for us. You see him with other teachers outside the class, and he almost passes for normal," Nelson Flower said. "There's just an occasional tic up under one eye to give him away."

"What's *your* class identity?" I asked him.

"I'm an anorexic who's slowly starving to death."

"At least you're a male," I said.

"He calls me Anna Rexy, though."

I slowed up because Nelson Flower was huffing and puffing to keep up with me. He was short, besides being fat, and he had tight little red curls, and a freckled face.

26

"Your family opened the new restaurant, hmm?"

"That's right."

"German food?"

"How'd you know that?"

"My mother heard it was German food. . . . Sauerbraten, schnitzel, strudel?" He was practically drooling.

"Homemade bratwurst," I said, "Königsberger klops, cider-cured hasenpfeffer."

"Neat!" he said. "We'll be out for dinner one night."

Piddle's class was the last class of the day, and after I said so long to Nelson Flower, I got my down vest out of my locker and stopped to look at the activities bulletin board in the front hall.

There was a huge poster announcing tryouts for *Our Town* by Thornton Wilder.

I was staring up at it when she came up behind me.

"Why don't you try out for Tall Man?" she said. "You're tall, Henry."

She was wearing a down vest, too, with a Fair Isle sweater under it, and a turtleneck sweater under that. She had on a pair of corduroy Levi's, Bean boots, and a navy-blue grosgrain hairband holding back the long coal-colored hair.

"I'm not an actor," I said.

"You don't have to be, to be Tall Man. Tall Man just has a few lines. He's not even onstage. He speaks up from the audience."

27

"Why would I want to be Tall Man?"

"You could meet my grandmother then. My grand-mother said you said someday she'd meet you."

"Does your grandmother come to school plays?"

"She does when I'm in them. I'm going to be Emily in this one."

"Is that the lead?"

"That's the lead . . . or one of them, anyway."

"Why should I just have a few lines and not even be onstage when you're the lead?"

"Because the big parts are already taken, Henry. . . . Mr. Piccara, the drama teacher, is down in Room 405 right now, waiting to cast Tall Man."

"Listen," I said, "I didn't know your father was Al Kiss. I'm sorry about that."

"You're sorry he's my father?"

"Don't start all that," I said. "I'm trying to be serious."

"Don't start all what?"

"All that smart talk. I'm trying to be serious."

"I want you to be serious," she said. "That's why I'm telling you to try out for Tall Man. We can be serious together, at rehearsals nights."

"Nights?" I said, with a little quiver working its way out of my blood and into my voice.

"Nights, Henry," she said, walking away. Then over her shoulder, with one of those slanted smiles, "Nights."

"Hey, Val!" someone in a parka shouted at her. "Come on!"

I watched her go out the front door with him.

Then I asked a kid coming toward me how to get to Room 405.

4

Dear Henry,

The reason I threw the ring out the window of the taxi was the way you announced this isn't an engagement ring or anything like that, it's just a ring. I knew it was just a ring. When I said I wanted a ring that was all I wanted—a ring! I wouldn't be making plans to go to college if I was engaged to be married, and I am only seventeen as you well know. A little young to be engaged to anyone, even you, Henry Schiller!

So I hated the way you had to be sure I didn't think it was an engagement ring, and I tossed it out the window because you made me really furious! I hope if you get involved with someone else you learn to be more sensitive, because as it is you're a conceited creep! It is too bad because I really, really cared a lot about you, but you did not even think of my plans to go to Bard and be a film director! You just got into a panic because I wanted a ring!

Good luck with your new life and forget all about me!

Lena

P.S. You have good taste in rings. It was beautiful.

I put Lena's letter aside and watched my mother try on a new dress.

My mother was blond and blue eyed, really pretty, but beginning to worry about wrinkles and gray hairs.

"Do I look too fat in this, Henry?" she asked me.

"No, you look nice." She did, too. It was another white dress—my mother lived in a white dream: dresses were white, rugs were, furniture was, drapes, even her piano downstairs in the restaurant.

My father'd never been as good-looking as she was, and I'd never figured out how the two of them had gotten together. My father had been half bald, with a paunch. He'd been on the gruff side, except for the few times she'd get him to take off his apron and join her in a song.

The customers loved it when he came out of the kitchen, and the two of them sang *"Muss I' Denn"* together, and "How Can I Leave Thee?"

31

But getting my father to do it was like pulling teeth. Even in the photographs we had of him he was wearing his long blue apron, with one of his short-sleeved white shirts, black pants, and black shoes.

There was a big picture of him framed on our living-room wall, standing in front of Peter's in Yorkville, with the restaurant sign behind him and *PETER HANS SCHILLER—Küchenmeister* printed across it in gold.

"You're sure this doesn't make me look fat?"

"I'm sure," I said. "Mom, when a woman is five months pregnant, what are some of the problems?"

"What?" She whirled around with her hands to her face. "Oh, no, Henry!" she said, before I could explain about Piddle's class. "That isn't what that letter from Lena is about?"

I told her about my Monday-morning class in Health and Human Behavior, and she sank into an armchair, with her eyes closed, murmuring, "Thank God!"

Then she laughed. "You're supposed to be a pregnant teenage girl?"

"Not supposed to be. I am. In that class."

"That's some class, Henry. . . . And what's this about acting in a play?"

"It's not a big part," I said.

"You never liked performing before."

"I never tried."

"I always thought sports was your thing."

"It is," I said. "I can do both."

"At least sports is during the day. We're going to need you at the restaurant nights, Henry."

"We won't start rehearsals for a few weeks, Mom. It won't take much of my time."

"I never thought of you liking to perform," she said. "I always thought you were like your father that way."

"I'm not much like him at all, Mom. Ernie and Fred are like him."

"I know," she said.

"I hate the restaurant business."

"I *know*, Henry, but you have to do something with your life."

"I'll figure something out," I said. So far the only thing I'd figured out was what I didn't want to do. That bothered me . . . a lot.

"Okay," my mother said. "In the fifth month there's a little movement . . . like a butterfly. There's some weight gain, too, but the greatest weight gain will occur in the sixth month."

"Am I sick in the morning?" I'd heard that somewhere.

"Not anymore," my mother reassured me.

The next day at school only Nelson Flower was calling me by name. I found out Valerie Kissenwiser was a senior, which explained why I didn't see her in any of my classes. I got only glimpses of her, and I glimpsed guys to the right and left of her; she was like the filling in a sandwich, with them the bread.

I ate alone, again, in the cafeteria. Nelson Flower told me he went home for lunch.

"Where do people like Valerie Kissenwiser go?" I asked him.

"She's part of that senior crowd who go to McDonald's in their cars," he said. "No one actually eats here unless they can't help it."

"I can't help it."

"Then you should bring your lunch. A lot of kids got ptomaine poisoning from the tuna-fish salad last spring, and almost died."

I made plans to pack some sandwiches the next day, and struggled through afternoon classes, beginning a letter to Lena in Contemporary History.

Dear Lena,

I never for a minute forgot you were going to be a film director, since you never let me forget it. But I don't want to fight. What I want is . . .

I didn't know what I wanted, and there the letter ended.

At Yorkville High, we'd been the ones everyone else watched, and we'd planned our entrances at games and dances a little late, so we'd hear them saying, "Hey, there's Henry and Lena!"

Lena'd even call me while she was dressing, to ask me what color sweater I was going to wear, or what color jacket, so she wouldn't wear anything that'd clash.

I used to make fun of her for doing it. I used to say, "Who cares what *we* wear, Lena?" as if that kind of stuff really bored me.

At the end of that school day, I was really feeling down, watching all the ones go two by two, and the ones in the cliques taking up the entire sidewalk so you couldn't get past them.

I was shuffling along behind a crowd like that, shivering in the cold, when Jody Kissenwiser caught up with me.

Her silver braces glistened in the late afternoon sun, and she dumped her books in my arms while she caught her breath, and zipped up her parka.

"Whew!" she said. "I thought you'd get away!"

"Where does your sister keep herself?" I said.

"How about starting with 'Oh, hello, Jody.'"

"Oh, hello, Jody."

"Hello, Henry." She took out a tube of Blistik and ran it along her lips.

"Where does your sister keep herself?" I said.

"I could get a complex, Henry. Here I am rushing to get to you, because you look really pathetic dragging down the walk all by yourself, and the first thing you ask me is where Val is."

"Just yesterday I got a letter from a girl who said I was really insensitive," I said.

"Are you bragging or complaining?"

"Apologizing. . . . How are you, Jody?"

"Okay. You want some Blistik?"

"No, thanks."

She put it back in her pocket and made a reach for the books she'd put in my arms.

"I'll carry them," I said. "Have you found a place to have your Sweet Sixteen party?"

"We're having it at Foo Chow's. They have great Pu Pu platters, and everything else out here closes down in the winter anyway."

"Was that guy your sister was with New Year's Eve her boyfriend?"

"I'll get to that, eventually," she said. "Do you want to buy me a Coke?"

"Sure."

"We'll go to Dirty Dottie's. We'll have to stand because all the nerds who don't have rides in cars get there too late to get booths."

"I don't mind standing."

"*I* mind it."

"Then let's go someplace else."

"After school you go to Dirty Dottie's around here."

"Dirty Dottie's it is," I said.

"It's really dirty, too. A pig wouldn't walk on that floor. I mind all the filth in there, too. I mind standing. I mind the filth. I mind being fifteen going on sixteen. And I mind being Val's sister."

"Why do you mind being Val's sister?" I didn't think "Val" suited her, and I made up my mind I'd never call her that. I'd call her Valerie.

"That fellow behind the bar at your place on New Year's—is he your brother?"

"Umm hmmm. Fred."

"Okay. Suppose every time you appeared in public, the first thing anyone said to you was 'Where's Fred?' "

"I apologized, Jody."

"I know you did. I'm not rubbing your nose in it. I'm just telling you what I have to put up with every time I appear in public."

"Maybe you should cut down on your public appearances."

"Oh ha ha. . . . It's the same way around the house when Our Hero's home. My father worships her. She can drown him in a teaspoon of water."

"Hey, Jody? I want to tell you something."

"I know. I know. You have the hots for my sister."

"That isn't what I want to tell you. I want to tell you that I didn't know Al Kiss was your father. I wouldn't have said anything if I'd known that."

"You can say anything you want, to me. I believe in being frank."

"I noticed. . . . But I didn't mean to be such a smartass. Sometimes when my mother's singing nights, someone will make a crack about her and it really gets me steamed."

"Was that your mother singing New Year's Eve?"

"Yeah. So I know what it's like when someone

makes fun of one of your parents."

"When Daddy's on, my sister sits there and suffers for him. Not me, though. It's his career, not mine. It's his and Val's career."

"They're close, hmmm?"

"Joined like scissors. Cut her, he bleeds. Punch him, she falls down."

"Will your sister be at Dirty Dottie's?"

"Will you shut up about my sister for two minutes?"

We walked a town block to a soda shop on Seaville's main street.

The sign outside didn't say Dirty Dottie's, just Dottie's. Inside, it was jammed with kids, and the old-fashioned jukebox was going full blast.

I got two Cokes at the counter, and stood over in a corner with Jody, my eyes on a search for her sister.

"Don't bother!" Jody shouted at me.

"Don't bother what?"

"Looking for her. She takes aerobic dancing Tuesday afternoons."

For a little while, the jukebox was silent.

"Okay," Jody said. "That wasn't her boyfriend New Year's Eve. It wasn't my boyfriend, either. It was our cousin with me, and his college roommate with Val. I think our cousin was trying to fix Val up with him, but it would *never* work!"

"Why wouldn't it work?"

"Because he idolizes Daddy. All he talked about

the whole evening was Daddy."

"What's wrong with that? Valerie idolizes him, too, doesn't she?"

"No one ever calls her Valerie."

"Doesn't she idolize your father, too?"

"Yes, she does. But she wants to be liked for herself, not because he's her father."

"Oh," I said.

"Get it?"

"Yeah. You want to be liked for yourself. She wants to be liked for herself."

"You got it," Jody said. "People are like onions."

"Hmmm?" I thought she'd said people were like onions.

"I said people are like onions. You have to peel back layer after layer. That's why I'm going to be a famous psychoanalyst someday."

"What's Valerie going to be?"

"Can you stick to *me* for two seconds?"

"I'm sorry."

"Whoever wrote you that letter is right."

"So you're going to be a shrink?"

"Don't say shrink. That's demeaning. Say psychoanalyst."

"Psychoanalyst."

"Val will probably go into publishing or write a book. What about you?"

"Oh, I'll be a molecular biologist, possibly. Possibly a weather girl."

"If you ever meet my father, don't ever let him know," Jody said.

"Don't ever let him know what?"

"Don't ever let him know that you don't know what you want to be," she said. "He hates boys who don't have any ambition."

"I have plenty of ambition. I just don't know what I want to be."

"Make up something when you're talking to him. Tell him you want to be a physicist or an architect or something important."

"The first time I meet him?"

"The first time you meet him," Jody said firmly. "Jewish boys always know what they want to be when they're as old as you are."

"I'm not Jewish."

"There's that, too," Jody said.

5

Late Thursday afternoon, while I cut up the sausage, Ernie rolled out the pastry for sausage rolls.

We were watching the old movie *Psycho* on TV in the kitchen of Peter's, getting ready for the weekend people. Seaville is in the center of the Hamptons. Weekends New Yorkers come out to their second homes.

Peter's had a Friday night special: the T.G.I.F. plate (Thank God It's Friday). We were working on that.

"Did you ever see Al Kiss?" I asked Ernie.

" 'The whole world is Jewish—lemme tell you.' "

Ernie did a fair imitation of him. " 'Even the sun is called Sol.' "

"Yeah," I said, "and a Bar Mitzvah is a Jewish dude ranch. I guess he's been telling the same old jokes for years."

"His jokes should be collecting Social Security," Ernie said.

"He still gets around, though. Nightclubs. TV."

"Henry?"

"What?"

"Do me a favor, Henry . . . no. Do yourself a favor. Breathe for a while. Take long breaths of fresh air. Go down to the ocean—it isn't very far—look at the view, drink in the salt air, get the sun on your face."

"What are you talking about?"

"Don't get all wrapped up in another girl so soon."

"I'm not," I lied.

"Fred told me you're getting a thing on Kiss's daughter."

"I'm not getting a thing on her. Why do you have to make it sound like I'm growing a wart, or getting a fungus between my toes? A thing! What's a thing?"

"It's what you get on girls."

"I suppose you and Fred fall in love, but I get a thing."

"It's the way you go about it, Henry. You throw yourself at it like someone jumping into a fireman's net from a burning building. Right after you got out of Kelly Plante's clutches, you got into Lena's clutches, and now that you're out of Lena's clutches, what are you getting into?''

He was grabbing the sausages I was slicing and throwing them into rectangles of pastry, then rolling them over.

The murder scene in *Psycho* was coming up. "We all go a little mad sometimes," Tony Perkins was telling Janet Leigh.

"Yeah, we all go a little mad," Ernie said, "but you could use a breather, Henry. Life can be very pleasant when you're *not* in love, too. I'm not in love. I feel fine.''

"Why are you so excited about my interest in Valerie Kissenwiser?" I said.

"Because we don't want you to go around the bend again. We've got to get Peter's off the ground. We need all of you, Henry. We can't afford to share you with a new obsession.''

"She's just this girl.''

"VK VK VK VK. Just this VK. Those are the initials you doodled all over one of our new menus last night. In ink!''

"Where is it? I'll erase it with some Liquid Paper.''

"Henry, I'm not worried about one menu. I'm trying to tell you something from my own experience. Take it easy. Give yourself some room. You don't need to go two by two all the time in this life. There's no flood, and we're not animals on our way into Noah's ark. Get to know yourself.''

"I'm not a loner like you, Ernie."

"You're going to end up like poor Fred, if you're not careful."

My brother Fred got married when he was nineteen. Second only to my father's being shot down, Fred's marriage was considered the family disaster.

Fred and his wife were the couple you saw eating out, without a single word to say across the table. Before they got married, Fred tried to cut his wrists once because she said she was going to date around. Now they didn't even share the same bedroom. Angel said that Fred's snoring kept her awake.

Valentine's Day, Fred always gave me some money and said get a valentine for Mom from me and one for Angel. I'd ask him if he wanted a mushy one for Angel or what? Or what, he'd tell me, but get Mom a mushy one—the big, oversized kind, okay?

Before they got married, he'd say, Henry, it's almost Valentine's Day. I'm asking you and Ernie to keep your eyes open for anything in the shape of an angel, anything with an angel on it. My Angel loves angels.

They sat around now in their rented house with her angel collection all over the living room, him with his nose buried in the newspapers—her watching *I Love Lucy* reruns on TV, laughing until she cried into a Kleenex.

"I'm not going to end up like Fred," I said.

"Don't. Be a romantic, instead. You know what

the trick to being a romantic is, Henry?"

"Having a style all your own." I said back what he'd told me.

"Right, right."

"In everything you do with a girl, from dancing to lighting her cigarette."

"Right, right. . . . But the most important thing is to come close to doing everything with her, but not too soon. Traveling is the best part, Henry. Arriving can be a little disappointing."

I didn't think I had to worry about having it all too soon, with Valerie Kissenwiser. I had to worry more about having it at all.

"I don't know if she likes you or not," Jody told me in Dirty Dottie's the next afternoon, after school. (Valerie was at cheerleaders' practice.) "I brought up your name like you said to, and she said did I know who Peter was? She meant does your family own Peter's, or does your family just run Peter's for Peter, I think."

"It's our place," I said.

"I said I thought it was your place. I said you bought me a Coke."

"You didn't say I asked a lot of questions about her?"

"I said you called her Valerie. That's all I said. She said Gawd, nobody ever calls me Valerie."

"Was she pleased that I call her Valerie?"

"She just said Gawd, nobody ever calls me Valerie. Daddy calls her Valley, like she's a piece of low land lying between hills."

"What does your mother call her?" I was getting my daily Valerie Kissenwiser fix, like an addict who can't get enough of his favorite drug.

"Mummy calls her Dear. She can't bear to say her name."

"Why?"

"Because she can't stand her. Daddy comes through the front door, tosses Mummy something gift wrapped in a box, then right away begins with 'Where's my tweet Valley pussums?' It's really pretty nauseating."

"Is she jealous of Valerie?"

"Oh! Oh! Oh! My eyes are tearing as we peel away another layer of the onion. Yes, she's jealous. All he cares about is Val and golf. There used to be a third passion: cards. But he lost so much money, my grandmother had to bail us out. My mother hates that—it's her great humiliation, second only to playing second fiddle to Val."

"Speaking of—" I said, and my whole body turned to stone one second, the second after, fire.

Valerie Kissenwiser was walking the length of Dirty Dottie's, in a Tyrolean jacket with silver buttons, a plaid skirt, and boots.

She had on her slanted smile, and when she got close she said, "I'm double-parked out front."

"So what?" Jody said. "I'm drinking a Coke."

"What are you doing, Henry?"

"I was just explaining the theory of relativity to your sister."

"If there's anything that bores me more than one of Einstein's old theories," Jody said, "it's my sister's come-ons."

I looked down shyly at Valerie. "Oh? Is that what this is?"

"Come on, Henry," she said. "That's what this is."

Outside, the snow was starting to come down again, and I hurried into the passenger seat of the white Riviera convertible.

"I hope Jody doesn't mind," I said.

"She likes being my foil. She knew I was coming by to get you."

"She didn't say anything about it."

"I told her not to. Don't you like surprises?"

"Yes, I like surprises."

"And I wore my Tyrolean coat for you. It's the closest thing to anything German I have."

"Well, thanks. Where are we going?"

"I'm going to drop you off. You can use a ride, can't you?"

"Yes. Thanks."

"I hear you're going to be Tall Man in the play?"

"If I can ever memorize the part," I said. Tall

Man's part was three lines: 1. Is there no one in town aware of— 2. Is there no one in town aware of social injustice and industrial inequality? 3. Then why don't they do something about it?

"I'll help you," Valerie said.

She turned on the windshield wipers. It was a wet snow I was hoping wouldn't stick and discourage the Friday-night travelers from New York.

"I admit I have an ulterior motive for driving you to Peter's. Besides the fact I like your face."

"I like your face, too."

"I know you do. I knew we liked each other's faces from the beginning. I had to bite my lip to keep from grinning back at you—remember? When you were trying to tell me all the things you could fix instead of German food? We can do fish. We can do lobster." She laughed. "We can do frogs' legs."

"We can do goulash," I said, "or goose."

She laughed again. "Uh. My name is Henry Schiller. Uh. I just moved to Seaville. You were cute, Henry. I had to bite my lip to keep from grinning."

"What's your ulterior motive?"

"Oh, I see. Compliments make you uncomfortable."

"Only when someone's said she has an ulterior motive for driving me home."

"Daddy's coming tonight," she said. "Do you know what his favorite thing in the whole world is?"

48

"It's you, according to your sister."

"It's me, and then it's strudel. Daddy loves good strudel."

"You want me to steal another strudel?"

"I'll pay for it."

"I'll steal it."

"Then if you're going to steal it, maybe you should come to dinner tomorrow night and meet Daddy."

"Maybe I should," I said.

"About seven-thirty? You can meet my grand-mother, too. My grandmother always said you said someday she'd meet you."

We bantered back and forth that way while we headed down the Montauk Highway toward Peter's.

I was getting sick to my stomach imagining Ernie's face, Fred's, my mother's, when I announced I had a Saturday-night dinner date, our first real Saturday night in business.

I was watching her in profile, that long soft black hair, the little smile tipping her mouth, and she'd actually invited me to her house.

She was telling me her grandmother already had a nickname for me. "That's a sign of affection, wouldn't you say, Henry?"

"What does she call me?"

"She calls you 'From The Restaurant.' She heard Jody and me talking and she wanted to know if we were talking about 'From The Restaurant.' "

Valerie looked across at me, smiling. "I told her I was going to ask From The Restaurant for dinner."

We were driving into Peter's.

"Valerie—" I began.

She said, "That's another thing I like, Henry. I like it that you call me Valerie. You're the only one who does."

"Valerie," I managed, "I can't come to dinner tomorrow night. I really wish I could, but I have to work."

She stopped the car and kept the motor running.

"I'll still steal you a strudel," I said. "I'll go inside now and get you one. Cherry?"

"No, don't," she said. "I can't accept another stolen strudel, if you can't come to help eat it."

"I can't."

"Can you come Sunday, for brunch?"

"That I can do."

"Then do that."

"Great!" I said. I started to get out of the car.

Valerie said, "Henry?"

"What?"

"I like it that you said yes first, even though you knew you had to work."

"I lost my head."

"I know it. That's what I like."

"I'll see you Sunday. What time?"

"Noonish?"

"Noonish. With the strudel," I said. "And my head."
I got out of the car, then leaned in and grinned at her.

She threw me a two-fingered kiss.

"I can't wait until Sunday, Henry," she said.

I couldn't either.

6

"I have to warn you that Daddy isn't in a good mood," Valerie said.

She'd met me at the door in a two-piece bright-orange rubber rain suit, with a matching hat that tied under her chin, and Bean rubber boots.

I'd arrived at the rambling three-story white wooden house promptly at noon. She opened the door herself, took the box with the strudel in it, and placed it on the front hall table. Then she led me out the door, and up a side path that went toward the ocean.

It was a bitter cold morning and I wasn't really dressed for a walk on the beach. I was wearing my best suit, a gray pinstripe, with a white broadcloth shirt, red-and-white-striped tie, and black loafers. I'd expected to go right from the Jeep to the inside of the house, so I had no coat on, only Ernie's black cashmere scarf to keep the cold wind off my neck.

We were holding hands as we headed up toward the dunes, a wet, salt spray hitting our faces.

"Daddy had a really bad week," Valerie continued. "Did you ever hear of an entertainer called Al Viss?"

"No."

"Neither had Daddy. He's some kind of Elvis Presley impersonator. Al Viss. El-vis, get it?"

"Yeah." She didn't have on any makeup and she looked really great.

She said, "Daddy got booked into some club in Philadelphia for a one-nighter. They made a mistake. They thought they were getting this Elvis Presley impersonator. There were all these middle-aged women with Al Viss signs. This Al Viss has some kind of following in Philadelphia, women and little girls wearing Al Viss T-shirts with gold crowns on them, and gold guitars, all carrying teddy bears."

"Why the teddy bears?"

"Elvis Presley loved teddy bears, I guess. Anyway, it was awful for Daddy. He was ready to do his shtick and they were expecting someone who'd dance around with a guitar singing 'Tutti Frutti.' "

We got to the top of the dunes and she let go of my hand so abruptly that I gave her a look.

"Daddy's probably watching us," she said. "He can see us now. Henry?"

"What?"

"I have to explain something to you."

"Okay."

"Things are happening sort of fast between us."

"Uh . . ." I couldn't deny the way I felt but I was surprised to hear her announce it.

"Don't 'uh' me. They are. I mean, nothing's happened but something's happening. Okay?"

"Okay," I said.

"And I just want to warn you that I'm always going to be a little strange acting anywhere where Daddy can see me. He's probably watching us out his bedroom window."

I gave a little wave over my shoulder. "Hi, Daddy!"

"It isn't funny," she said. "He just affects me that way."

"Well, thanks for warning me."

"And he's in such a bad mood because of what happened in Philadelphia, and because of Vivienne being here, too."

"Who's Vivienne?"

"My cousin. Vivienne Trump. She's only three but she really gets on Daddy's nerves. She's from my mother's side of the family, like my grandmother is, and that side of the family depresses Daddy."

"Doesn't your grandmother live with you?"

"You might say we live with her." She waved her

hand in a semicircle. "This is all Grandmother Trump's. We used to live in New York City but—"

"Hey! So did I!"

"But we've been living out here since Grandfather Trump died."

"Where did you live in New York?" I asked her.

We talked about New York for a while, walking down along the hard sand by the ocean.

She told me her father had been going through some bad years, that everybody thought he was this big star with no worries, but he wasn't getting anywhere near the work he'd once gotten.

"We had to cut down a whole lot on our life-style," she said.

She didn't mention anything about gambling.

I let her talk. I decided not to parade our family problems at the same time.

I was trying to adjust to this new, serious Valerie Kissenwiser, and to keep from taking her hand, or putting my arm around her.

I was also trying to keep warm, and by the time we got back to the big white house, my ears were bright red and ringing from the dampness, and my nose was running.

"You look like you've been crying, Henry," Jody Kissenwiser greeted me in the front hall, while Valerie hung up her jacket. She pulled a wad of Kleenex out of the pocket of her jeans and handed me one. "Did Val tell you Daddy's in a bad mood?"

I nodded and blew my nose.

"Remember, when he asks you what you want to be, say an architect or something impressive."

"If he asks me, I'll think of something impressive," I said.

"Oh, he'll ask you," she promised. "Gee, you got all dressed up. With your red nose and that suit on, you look like you've come from a funeral."

"I feel like I'm going to one," I told her. "My own."

There were seven of us at the table, under the crystal chandelier in the dining room.

Al Kiss sat at one end, wearing a tattersall shirt, so bald I realized that on television he wore a thin-haired toupee.

On one side of him was Mrs. Trump, a little white-haired woman in a black dress, who hadn't shown any sign she knew how to smile.

Opposite her was Valerie's mother, lots of makeup, blond, wearing gold earrings and a gold necklace, very tanned for the middle of winter, and not a talker.

Next to her was little sunny-haired Vivienne, who was playing with her food instead of eating it, and who left the table every time the telephone rang. It rang three times while we were at the table. Jody seemed to be the official Sunday afternoon answerer of the telephone, which was just outside the dining room. Next to it was a tiny red play telephone, which

Vivienne went to answer when Jody answered the real one.

Jody would say, "I'm sorry. We're having brunch. Can he call you?"

Vivienne would say, "I'm torry. We having bwunch. Can he call you?"

Jody and Valerie were flanking me, as I sat at the other end of the table. Under the table, curled into a ball, was Nachus, a declawed Siamese cat.

For a while, everyone just ate. The night before, Nelson Flower and five members of his family had come into Peter's and ordered practically everything on the menu, but the Kissenwisers' brunch had twice as many dishes as we'd carried out to the Flowers.

What conversation there was didn't include me, for a long time.

Mrs. Trump's favorite exclamation was "Hoo-ha!"

I found out that it could mean anything.

When Al Kiss complained about his agent's booking him into that club in Philadelphia, Mrs. Trump said, "Some agent!" indignantly. "Hoo-ha!"

When little Vivienne toddled toward her little phone after the big phone rang, Mrs. Trump said with admiration, "Is she smart that tyke? Hoo-ha!"

When she bit into the smoked salmon, she said to Valerie's mother, "Did you buy this out here?" surprised. "Hoo-ha!"

"ACH-CHOO!" from Al Kiss suddenly. "Nachus

is in the room! Am I wrong? ACH-CHOO! You want I should die of an allergy? Get her out!" . . . But Nachus did not need any invitation to leave. She was on her way out from under the table, giving a look in the direction of the sneeze, tail flagging. She gave a little hiss and left.

"I need to live with a cat who hisses me?" Al Kiss asked the ceiling.

Near the end of the meal, he finally addressed me. "You eat like a bird."

Little Vivienne thought that was pretty funny. She giggled and said, "You eat like a wobin." She actually had on a hair ribbon. I didn't think I'd ever seen one before except in pictures.

"It's very good, though," I said. "When you have a restaurant and you're around food all the time, you don't eat a lot at the table."

"You eat like a 'parrow," little Vivienne said. She was mashing some cream cheese down into a bagel with the back of her fork.

"Is that your family's restaurant? Peter's?" Al Kiss asked me.

"Yes."

"That was good strudel," Mrs. Trump said.

"Very good," Al Kiss agreed. "So you're in the restaurant business?"

"My family is," I said. "I help out." I stole a look at Jody. "But I probably won't stay in the business."

"No? Why not?" Al Kiss said.

"Well, it's not a very good . . . it's not a real profession," I said.

"It's a poo!" Al Kiss said.

"Sir?"

"I said it's a poo!"

"Uncle Al said 'poo,' " Vivienne told her grand-mother.

"He didn't mean poo-poo, darling," her grand-mother said.

"Daddy calls a poor-opportunity occupation a poo," Valerie explained. Under the table she ran the toe of her Bean boot up my pant leg.

"That's what it is, all right," I agreed. "Particularly out here."

"So why'd you come out here?" Al Kiss said.

"My brothers decided to come out here. My broth-ers run the business since my father died."

"That's a business where a man dies young," Al Kiss said. "That's a killer."

"My father was shot to death," I said.

"Oh, Hen-ry," Valerie said. "You never told me that."

"The business didn't kill him. He was killed in a stickup."

"That's the business," Al Kiss said. "Stickups are part of the business."

" 'Tick 'em up!" Vivienne pointed her thumb and her first finger at me.

"Darling," Mrs. Trump told her, "never play stick

'em up. Never. It's not a little girl's game. . . . She gets that from television," Mrs. Trump said.

"So what do *you* plan to be, Henry?" Al Kiss said.

"Something like a brain surgeon," I said. It just came out that way.

"Something like a brain surgeon?" Al Kiss began wiping his mouth with his napkin as though he was wiping away rubber cement from his lips. He was staring at me.

"Something like that," I said feebly. "A doctor of some kind."

Valerie's boot left my leg and she changed the subject, fast, as though she was embarrassed for me.

"Henry and I are going to be in the school play together."

"Acting!" her father said. "That's another poo. Show business today is the pits!"

"I don't want to be an actor," I said. "I've only got three lines in the play."

"What play is that?" Valerie's mother spoke up.

"*Our Town*, Mother," Valerie said. "I only told you about a hundred times that I'm playing Emily in *Our Town*."

"Is it a big role, Valley? I don't remember the play," Al Kiss said.

"It's one of the leads, Daddy."

"That's my girl. . . . What are you playing?" he asked me.

"Tall Man," I said.

"You don't have a name?"

"I'm just playing a tall man who speaks up from the audience."

"Something like a tall man, huh?" he laughed. "The role just grabbed you, hah?" He gave another guffaw, and Valerie rushed to the rescue.

She said, "I think all the rehearsals we'll go to together nights grabbed Henry." Her face got bright red. She knew that would get him, but she'd gone ahead and said it anyway, so I wouldn't look like a wimp who'd go out for a nothing role in a play, for no reason.

Al Kiss was thinking it over, frowning. Valerie's boot was back up under my trouser leg.

"How old are you, Henry?" Al Kiss said.

"Seventeen."

"A senior?"

He knew how to hurt. "A junior," I said.

"A junior in the senior play?" he said.

"It's a school play," Valerie said, "not a senior play."

"When I went to school," Al Kiss said, "some of the senior boys dated junior girls, but not the other way around. Senior girls never dated juniors."

"Oh, Daddy," Valerie said.

"I'm just telling you how it was when I went to school."

"There's no standards anymore," Mrs. Trump said. "Standards went out the window."

61

"Valerie here will probably be going off to Antioch next year, Antioch, Ohio State, one of those colleges," Al Kiss said.

"Oh, *Daddy*," Valerie said.

"Where will you be going in two years, Henry?"

"Maybe Yale," I said. "Maybe Harvard," I said. "Someplace like that."

"Someplace like that to be something like a brain surgeon," he said.

"Hoo-ha!" Mrs. Trump said under her breath.

The telephone rang and little Vivienne and Jody made a dive for the other room.

"A young boy dreams he's on a ship at sea," Al Kiss said, "and the ship has begun to sink. It's possible, however, for the boy to save himself and one other person, either his mother or his father. But not both. What should he do, Henry?"

"Uh."

"Well?"

I tried to figure out what he wanted to hear.

"Do you want me to tell you what he should do, Henry?"

"Why don't you tell me what he should do, sir?"

"I'll tell you what he should do. He should wake up!"

Mrs. Trump was nodding her head in agreement.

"There's a moral in that somewhere," said Al Kiss.

From the other room, Jody was saying, "We're having brunch."

"We having bwunch,"—Vivienne.

62

7

"Who's pregnant this afternoon?" Piddle barked out as he lumbered into the classroom. "Stand, state your name and the month."

"Henry Schiller," I said, scrambling to my feet. "January."

Piddle slammed his books down hard on his desk. I stood there quaking in my Top-Siders.

"Mr. Schiller," Piddle shouted. "Come forward and face the class!"

Piddle's brown suit looked like it had never been taken to the cleaners, or never been taken off while Piddle slept nights.

All Piddle's exposed skin was red, as though the

63

hot blood coursing through his veins was ready to burst from his skin. His brown hair was thin, flat on his big head, and combed forward in greasy bangs.

"Repeat your answer," Piddle said to me as I stood before the class.

"Henry Schiller. January."

"Mr. Schiller," Piddle began, "is it your opinion that I have not availed myself of a calendar, that I do not have access to a daily newspaper, that I cannot remember some weeks back to when there was a Christmas tree, as well as a Hanukkah menorah, in the front lobby of this high school?"

"I don't know what you're getting at, Mr. Peddle."

"What I'm getting at, Mr. Schiller, is *not* what month it is now!" Piddle bellowed. "I know the month, and the year, and the day! What I'm getting at is the month of your pregnancy!"

"The fifth month, sir."

"The second trimester, hmmm?"

"Yes, sir. I opted to have the baby."

"Kindly opt to tell the class how you feel?"

"Well, I'm trying to eat high-protein foods and—"

Piddle cut me off. "I did not ask about your diet, Mr. Schiller! I asked how you feel."

"I feel g-good," I stammered.

"No one is interested in your frame of mind," said Piddle. "If you had a mind at all, you would not be in your present condition! So concentrate on your

64

body. How does your body feel? *What* does your body feel?"

"Movement," I began remembering what my mother'd told me. "A little movement . . . like a butterfly. There's some weight gain, too, although the greatest weight gain will occur in the sixth month."

"Don't get ahead of yourself, Mr. Schiller!" Piddle roared.

"I don't throw up anymore," I offered.

When he was finished with me, I went back down the aisle. He went back behind his desk. He picked up a ruler and began tapping it on the desk top as I sat down. "Is Mr. Schiller experiencing the heartbeat yet? Anyone?" Beat, beat, beat with the ruler.

I remembered the way Valerie had pushed me against my locker that morning, crooning in her husky voice, "Two hearts that beat as one, Henry. Isn't it thrilling?"

"Yours and mine," I said into her long black hair.

"Yours and your baby's," she said. I'd told her that on Monday afternoons I was a pregnant teenage girl.

"Not yet," I said.

"Oh, yes, at eighteen to twenty weeks, lover boy."

"Anyone?" Piddle demanded again. "Mr. Schiller?"

"Yes," I said. "I'm experiencing the heartbeat."

Piddle saved his greatest cruelty for the very end of class, for Nelson Flower.

He marched himself down to Nelson Flower's desk and poked him in the belly with the ruler.

I figured Nelson Flower had just about digested the sausage rolls he'd devoured at Peter's on Saturday, the Wiener schnitzel, potato dumplings, Königsberger klops, sauerkraut, sauerbraten, on and on.

"Mr. Flower." Piddle had a really mean smile on his face. "What are you weighing in at this afternoon?"

"Ninety-four pounds, sir." Times three, I figured.

"And as emaciated as you are, you still feel *what*, Mr. Flower?"

"Fat, sir."

"Yes, fat!" Another poke in the belly. "That is symptomatic of the anorexic. No matter your weight, you feel FAT!"

Nelson Flower looked like he was ready to bawl.

He was saved by the bell.

"FAT, Anna Rexy!" Piddle yelled at him, and Nelson Flower made a break for the door, waddling as fast as his short, plump legs could carry him.

I looked for him when I got out into the hall, but he'd disappeared. I'd wanted to commiserate with him. He was the only guy who ever went out of his way to talk to me.

I didn't spend much time trying to find him.

I had a date in a white Riviera convertible, waiting for me behind the school, in the parking lot.

———

"Nineteen parents once signed a petition to try and stop that class," Valerie told me in the car. "Jeffry Formento's mother tried to sue Piddle because Piddle gave him the identity of a herpes victim."

"Why is he so mean?"

"He's mean," she shrugged. "He finally changed Jeffry to a case of chronic acne. Jeffry Formento! With skin like a newborn baby!"

"Please," I said, "let's not talk about newborn babies."

We were heading down the driveway when I spotted Nelson Flower coming out the back door of school.

"There's Nelson now," I said.

"I see him. He's hard *not* to see."

"Valerie?"

"What?"

"Can we offer him a ride?"

She pulled over and I rolled down the window. I shouted out, "Do you want a ride?"

Nelson Flower looked behind him, then back at the car. He pointed to himself and mouthed, "Me?"

"You," I said.

He came toward the car wearing this big grin. I opened the door and moved over very close to the smell of summer flowers.

"Closer," Valerie told me.

"He's got room."

"Closer, Henry. Closer."

I asked him if he was on his way to Dirty Dottie's.

"I never go there," he said, pulling the car door shut. "I only like Sedutto ice cream or Hershey's, and I don't like Hershey's unless it's chocolate marshmallow. Dirty Dottie makes her own ice cream and there's always a lot of ice chips in it."

"I like Häagen-Dazs," Valerie said.

"Only when it's vanilla," Nelson Flower said. "I don't like the other flavors. I like Bassett's, too, but you can't buy it out here. I sometimes like Breyer's butter almond."

We talked about ice cream and chocolate truffles (Krön's were the best, Nelson said) until we got to the light at Main Street and Maritime Lane.

"I get off here," Nelson said. "I live on Maritime."

He eased himself out of the car, then ducked his head back inside before he shut the door. "Thanks!" he said. "I really mean it, too!"

I started to move away from Valerie but she grabbed my coat.

"Stay!" She smiled.

The sun was finally out in Seaville. I didn't ask Valerie where we were going. I didn't care where we went. We'd suddenly slipped into this easy thing together, as though we were a long-time couple, the way Lena and I had been at Yorkville High.

Sunday night I'd called her, and we'd stayed on the phone for an hour.

Her grandmother had answered the telephone. I heard her tell Valerie, "It's From The Restaurant."

I wondered if little Vivienne was telling her little telephone, "It's Fwom De Westwant."

I'd become philosophical about her family. You had to be philosophical about a girl's family. Lena's father'd called me Adolf, and shouted "Heil!" when I went to pick her up nights. Before that, Kelly Plante's mother wrote something on the back of her wallet identification card that she said Kelly should remember when she was out with me.

When I met him, I liked him.
When I liked him, I loved him.
When I loved him, I let him.
When I let him, I lost him.

Philosophy helped you get past girls' families.

"You know where my grandmother is this afternoon?" Valerie said.

"Where?"

"In Bellport. My uncle came for little Vivienne and took my grandmother back with them. . . . Do you know where my mother is?"

"Where?"

"My mother is at Chez Joey having a permanent. . . . Do you know where my father is?"

"Where?"

"My father's caught the three o'clock jitney into New York. He's going to be on *Live at Five* tomorrow afternoon."

"I know where Jody is," I said.

"Right. Jody is at Dirty Dottie's per usual. So the coast is clear, Henry."

She turned onto Ocean Avenue.

I decided to keep my mouth shut. I didn't want to take the chance of saying anything that could possibly steer her from the course I had a feeling we were on.

I watched the houses along Ocean Avenue get farther and farther apart as we drove toward the end.

"You know what I like about you, Henry?"

"You said you liked my face."

"Your face and what you just did for Nelson Flower. That's something Daddy would have done."

"*You* did it. You stopped the car."

"I wouldn't have done it if you hadn't suggested it. I'm not naturally kind, Henry. I'll tell you that about myself right now. I like being kind, but it doesn't come naturally to me. Daddy's kind. I know we make jokes that the cat hisses at him, but he's a cream puff. People don't know that about him, but he believes in Maimonides."

"What's Maimonides?"

"Not what. *Who.* He was this famous philosopher," Valerie said, and the big white wooden house was coming into view. My heart was starting to go faster.

"Maimonides," Valerie said, "believed one of the greatest acts of charity is helping somebody out without other people knowing about it. . . . Daddy does that all the time. The people he helps out sometimes don't even know about it. That's Maimonides, too. Daddy follows Maimonides because he says Maimonides knows how to lend a helping hand."

We were turning into the circular driveway in front of the white wooden house.

"Daddy might not come off as a deep thinker," Valerie said, "but he really is. . . . What's more, he's a softy like you are, Henry." She flashed me a smile, and turned the key off, stopping the motor.

"Are you nervous?" she said.

"Why would I be nervous?" I said. I was a wreck inside.

"Why would *I* be?" Valerie said. "I am, though."

We got out of the car and went up the walk in the sun.

"Daddy never locks doors," she said.

"Does Maimonides believe you should leave your doors open?"

"Daddy says anyone who gets this close to the house, and can't get in, will just break in." We went through the door.

Once it was shut, I reached for her.

"No," she said. "Unh-uh. First we get out of our coats. Then we put on some music. Henry?"

"W-what?" My voice was giving away the fact I was crumbling into little pieces under my skin.

"The first time we kiss has to be special. Because we're special." She turned around, still in her coat, and looked at me. "Aren't we special?"

"We're special," I said softly.

She moved a little closer to me. "If we're so special," she said, "what are we waiting for?"

She had ahold of my coat again, then my mouth.

"Oh, Henry," she murmured after we'd kissed for a long time, "Henry . . . I wish you'd take my coat off."

I started to let go of her, to help her off with her coat.

She said, "No. I wish you'd take my coat off without going away."

I started fumbling with the buttons while she kept one hand on my neck and her mouth against mine.

"Oh, Henry," she said into my nose.

"Valerie," I whispered back. I was getting the coat off her shoulders and she was saying, "Henry . . . Henry."

"Let me take your coat now," I said.

"Just let it fall on the floor," she said.

She moved so her arms were out of it, and it slid to the black-and-white marble floor.

"Oh, Henry," she said, and her hands were unzipping my duffel coat.

We were still mouth to mouth.

"I'm crazy about you!" I said. "Valerie?" We were eyeball to eyeball. "I'm so crazy about you!"

That was when Al Kiss's voice sounded. "Well! Isn't this astounding!"

He'd come around the corner, and he was standing

there in the hallway, his tassel loafers an inch away from Valerie's polo coat.

"Daddy!"

"Astounding!" Al Kiss said. He bent over and picked up Valerie's coat.

"How do you do, Mr. Kiss," I got out, and I could feel the blood go to my face.

"Astounding!" he said, shaking his head from side to side. "Just astounding when you miss your jitney what happens in your own front hall!"

Valerie was bright red, too, and dumbstruck.

"Your daughter and some shlemiel come through your front door in this big hurry, two kids, end of a school day. What's the rush, I'm wondering? Are they hot to help each other with their homework or what?"

"We aren't *kids*, Daddy," Valerie said. ". . . We were just going to play some tapes," weakly.

"Astounding! But the tapes are back there," waving his arm toward the living room. "And you're still in here. Apparently you just couldn't wait until you got in there."

"We would have gone in there," Valerie said.

"Astounding! You would have tripped over your coat on your way in."

"Daddy, what are you making so much of this for?" Valerie said in a little voice.

"Your grandmother's in Bellport! Your mother's at the beauty parlor! Your sister's not here! And I'm supposed to be on the jitney to New York!"

Neither Valerie nor I had anything to say to that.

"So the house is empty!" He was pointing a manicured finger at Valerie next. "You know a boy, a something like a brain surgeon, for something like a week, and you prance home with him as soon as the house is supposed to be empty! Astounding!"

"Sir," I began to say, but I didn't have any idea what I would have said, even if he'd let me say it.

"Don't sir me! What the hell is my daughter's good coat doing on the floor? Astounding!"

"Please stop saying 'astounding,' Daddy. It isn't that astounding."

"Millie and Tillie are two old girlfriends that meet for lunch," he said. "Millie tells Tillie she married a billionaire who's bought her a yacht, and Tillie says, Astounding! . . . Then Millie tells Tillie she's also got a jewelry box filled with emeralds, overflowing with diamonds. And Tillie says, Astounding! . . . And charge accounts in all the best stores I got, too, Millie says. And Tillie says, Astounding!"

Valerie and I just stood there while he continued.

"Finally Millie asks Tillie what she's been up to. . . . Tillie says she's been going to a charm school. . . . Millie asks her what she's learned there. . . . Well, Tillie says, they taught me to say 'Astounding!' instead of 'Bullshit!' "

Valerie let out her breath in a long sigh.

"You get the lead out of your shoes," Al Kiss said

to me. "The door's right behind you."

"We weren't," I began sputtering, "I wasn't, we didn't—"

"I said there's the door what's your hurry!" he shouted at me.

"Okay," I said, pulling the zipper back up on my duffel coat. "I'll see you, Valer—"

"Astounding!" Al Kiss shouted.

Where was good old Maimonides when I needed him?

8

Early Tuesday morning, my brother Fred called from his house to say a water pipe had broken. I went there to help him move out heavy furniture, and was so late for school, I missed seeing Valerie.

Right before lunch, I saw Jody in the hall. "Stop looking," she said. No hello. No how are you. "She went out to lunch with Himself. I'm eating lunch with Trevor (What a Face!) Feldman, or I'd eat with you."

I thought of how Valerie was always telling me she loved my face. "What is it with you Kissenwisers?" I said. "You're all face crazy."

"We're terrified of bodies, that's why."

Trevor Feldman was the shortest boy in the senior class. His own kid brother towered over him. But on stilts, he could have starred in his own TV series he was so good-looking. What was he up to with Jody?

She said, "I've got a roast beef sandwich I'm trying to trade half of for another kind. What have you got I can have half of?"

"I've got half a roast pork on pumpernickel."

"Yech! Ham I don't mind, but pork!" She stuck two fingers down her throat. "There's Trevor now. I always end up with half a peanut butter sandwich when I trade with one of the Feldmans."

"How are things at home?" I asked her before she got away.

"Do you want to go to Dirty Dottie's after school? Val has aerobics."

"I have to move furniture for my brother. Is your father in a bad mood?"

"He's started calling you Heinrich. It doesn't look good."

"We weren't doing anything."

"Yet," Jody said. "Here's a note from Val. I'd ask you to eat with Trevor and me, but we have highly personal stuff to talk about."

I bought myself some milk, and ate at a table in the back of the cafeteria, after I read the note from Valerie.

Dear Henry,

I looked for you this morning but couldn't find you anywhere. I have my dancing class right after last bell, so this is to tell you the latest. I probably made things worse for us with Daddy. He was furious and I tried to calm him down by saying I thought I was a little in love with you. Maybe I am, and maybe I'm not. We are still a maybe. But I thought Daddy would feel better about everything if I said that, since he's old-fashioned. Well, Henry, it made him all the madder is what it did. He says everything is going too fast, and I am not to date any boy exclusively. The only way I can date you, he says, is if I date other boys, too. Before I can date you again, he says, I have to date someone else. . . . But you have to work weekends, anyway, hmmm??? We can talk about this at play rehearsal Thursday night. Don't call for a while. Okay?

Love (maybe),
Valerie

P.S. Maybe more than maybe.
P.P.S. Daddy's going to be on Live at Five *this afternoon. He's taking me to lunch, then catching the jitney I wish he'd caught yesterday afternoon!*

After Fred finished moving the furniture back with me, he rushed off to Peter's to make Stuffed Cabbage Charlemagne, our Tuesday-night special.

I asked Angel if I could hang around to watch *Live at Five*.

"What do you want to watch a news show for?"

"It's news and interviews. They're interviewing this comedian."

"Your girlfriend's father?"

"Al Kiss," I said.

"So you're getting into something again, Henry."

"Angel, I'm just living. I'm not getting into something."

"Yeah, I'm just living, too. Every single piece from our conversation pit is soaking wet because your brother said just put a pan under the drip until we can get a plumber. . . . I'm just living, too."

We were sitting in folding chairs on the bare floor of their living room. Across from us, above the TV, there was a framed picture of an angel flying in the clouds, holding a harp. There was a stuffed angel drying out on a radiator cover, and an assortment of china angels on the windowsill.

Angel had black hair and brown eyes, and she was dressed in a red pantsuit. She said, "I usually watch a *Mary Tyler Moore* rerun at this hour."

"I'm sorry," I said.

"I don't really mind this time," she said. "I read in *TV Guide* this is the one when Georgette confides that Ted has taken to sleeping on the couch. I've seen it before."

"How can you watch those things twice?" I said.

"Because they're reruns, Henry. What am I supposed to do out here where I don't know anybody?"

"I don't know, Angel. . . . That's why I'm trying to meet new people."

"You just need a person, Henry. You don't need people. Just a girl."

"What's wrong with that?"

"You get too intense, Henry. I used to think Fred got too intense until I met you."

"Shhh!" I said. "They're doing the introduction."

"Your brother hasn't bought me an angel in a year. I had angels up the kazoo before we were married."

"They're hard to find out here. Shhhhh."

"I'm talking about a whole year! Not a month! Is that him?"

"Yeah. Listen, Angel."

Al Kiss was leaning back in a director's chair, doing a few dumb jokes about New York. Corny ones. "The Statue of Liberty carries a gun in this town" type jokes. The woman interviewing him wasn't laughing.

Then Al Kiss tried a few jokes about all the fast-food places cropping up in New York. "You know the kind of place I mean—where you can't get a job unless you've got a skin condition."

The interviewer said she'd noticed he wasn't doing any gambling jokes. Is it true, she wanted to know, that you suffered some heavy losses? Al Kiss looked uncomfortable. He said gambling was a sure way to

80

get nothing for something. . . . Do you want to discuss those losses? the interviewer said. Al Kiss just gave her a look, which made her uneasy, and she said, "Well, it's just that we don't know much about the *real* you, Al."

"Don't ask," he said. He was beginning to sweat.

"You have a daughter, is that right?"

"Daughters."

"How many?"

"Two," he said, and he was sitting forward suddenly, as though he'd just recovered from a hard punch. "One," he said, "is dating a young German storm trooper with ears so big he could pick up cable TV."

My hand went to one of my ears.

"Hen-ry!" Angel said.

"Heinrich," Al Kiss said. "Heinrich's got ears so big he could play Ping-Pong without a paddle."

The interviewer was laughing.

"Hen-ry!" Angel was gasping.

"Heinrich," Al Kiss said, "goes in an elevator, pushes the buttons, and looks for gum. . . . *Him* she loves?"

Ha Ha from the interviewer.

Al Kiss's face was lit up with this big smile. "When my daughter first brought him to the house, Heinrich asked my younger daughter how to talk to a Jewish girl. What do you say to one, he asks my youngest kid. So my youngest kid says that Jewish girls like to converse on three subjects—this is true—three subjects, she tells him: food, family, and philosophy. I'm coming downstairs a short time later and I hear Heinrich and my older daughter talking."

"Is this true, Henry?" Angel whispered.

"Shhhh! No!"

"Heinrich says to her—her name is Valerie. Heinrich says, Valerie, do you like sauerbraten? . . . My girl says no, she doesn't. He's covered food, so he goes on to family. He says, Valerie, do you have a brother? My girl says no, she doesn't. . . . Okay, on to philosophy. Valerie, he says, if you had a brother, would he like sauerbraten?"

The interviewer was laughing hilariously.

"*Him* she loves?" Al Kiss said.

"Thank you, Al Kiss," the interviewer said. "We enjoyed hearing a little about your life . . . *and* your daughter's—and *him* she loves?"

Angel got up to turn the dial to the *Mary Tyler Moore* show. "Hey, Hen-ry," she said, "he's talking about you on national television!"

I was still red.

"Is all that true?"

"Of course it isn't true!" I said. "Is my name Heinrich?"

"Pretty close," she said. "He shouldn't have said that about your ears, though. That's hitting below the belt."

There was a commercial break on TV. The local

Seaville station showed a man dressed as a pearl, coming out of a giant oyster shell. "For a pearl of a car, try Earl T. Farr. Farr Motors. Pantigo Road."

"Look, Henry," Angel said. "There's the local celebrity Fred says is always at Peter's."

"Who cares?" I muttered.

"Earl T. Farr. Fred says he's there a couple of nights a week."

"Angel," I said, "who cares whether someone who dresses up as a pearl on TV comes to Peter's?"

"Touchy," Angel said.

"Very," I agreed. "I didn't mind the Heinrich bit, but why did he have to zero in on my ears?"

"That's what I just said!" Angel said.

When I finally got back to Peter's there was a postcard waiting for me.

Dear Henry,

Of all things my family is planning to vacation in the Hamptons this summer. We'll be out, the weekend after this, staying at Seaville Cottages, to look for a summer place. Don't contact me there unless you are willing to see me just as

Your friend, Lena

9

The Seniors of Seaville High present the annual

DEAD OF WINTER DANCE
Saturday, the 16th of January
9:00 P.M.
in the gym.
Come as someone DEAD!
LIVE music from Ironing Bored!
Proceeds to the Senior Prom Fund!
SUPPORT YOUR SENIORS!

"Are you going to this thing?" I asked Nelson
Flower. We were studying the bulletin board in the

84

hall, outside Mr. Piccara's room.

"Sure, everybody goes to it. Aren't you going, Henry?"

"I don't know if I can get off work."

Nelson was chomping on some Nabisco bridge mix. We both had tiny roles in *Our Town*, and we'd ducked out of rehearsal while they were going through Act Two.

"Who are you going as?" I asked him.

"I'm going as the character I am in the play."

Nelson played Another Man from Among the Dead in *Our Town*.

His only line was "That's what they say."

"Why is everybody around here so caught up in the dead?" I said.

"It's just coincidence," he said. "We've never done *Our Town* before, but we've had the Dead of Winter Dance for three years in a row now."

"Are you taking someone?"

"I don't have anyone to take," he said. "I don't date yet."

We wandered back into Mr. Piccara's room, where Valerie was up in the front of the room reading Emily's lines.

"Good-bye. Good-bye, world. Good-bye, Grover Corners . . ."

"Val?" Mr. Piccara said. "It's *Grover's* Corners."

"Good-bye, Grover's Corners . . . Mama and Papa.

Good-bye to clocks . . . and Mama's sunflowers. And . . ."

"Val?" Mr. Piccara said. "It's Good-bye to clocks *ticking*."

"I'm sorry, Mr. Piccara."

Mr. Piccara said, "I think we'll call it a night. You're doing fine, Val, but I think we're all tired."

She was wearing a pair of beat-up jeans with a white shirt tucked into them, and a red corduroy vest. Her hair was tied back with a red ribbon.

"Are you waiting for her?" Nelson Flower asked me.

"Yeah. Do you need a ride?"

"Three's a crowd," he said. "I saw her father on TV day before yesterday. Are you supposed to be Heinrich?"

"I guess so," I said, and Valerie came up behind me and put her arms around my waist, hugging me.

"Hi, Nelson! Want a ride?"

"Thanks, anyway," he said. "I'll just walk and practice my line."

When we got in the car, Valerie said, "The minute you came back in the room, I got so nervous I blew all my lines, Heinrich."

"Not funny," I said. "I feel as if I ought to have an ear lift."

"I could *kill* Daddy! I thought the Heinrich part

86

was funny but I told him it was gross to pick on your poor ears."

"He just made it all up on the spot, didn't he?"

"He said it just came to him out of the blue. He was really up after the show. He called us to *kvell* and—"

"To what?"

"*Kvell*. That's Yiddish. It means to gush. He said at least you're good for something." She looked over at me and smiled. "Don't be mad, okay?"

"I'm not mad if he's not."

"He is, but he's also really high on this new '*him* she loves' bit. Daddy loves to be creative. He loves it when he comes up with something instead of mouthing what some writer gives him."

"Is it going to be a bit?"

"Is *it* going to be a bit!"

"Oh, *no*."

"I'll make you forget all about it, Henry."

"Starting when?"

"Almost immediately," she said. "It's only quarter to ten. I have until eleven."

Then she said, "Look in the backseat."

"What is it?"

"It's a picnic basket. We're on our way to Main Beach for a picnic in the car. I hope you're not hungry, because there's nothing to eat. It's not that kind of picnic."

"What kind of picnic is it?"

"You'll see."

You could hear the big waves pounding against the sand, and barely make out a ship's lights through the fog.

Valerie set up half a dozen small jars with candles inside and lighted them, fixing them along the dashboard. She put on a tape that played old songs like Chicago's "Hard to Say I'm Sorry," Patti Austin's "Baby, Come to Me," and Air Supply's "The One That You Love."

Then she took out two tiny bottles of Tía Maria.

"Daddy always gets these on airplanes," she said. "Fish out the glasses from the bottom of the basket, Henry."

There were two crystal brandy snifters. I held them out while she emptied the liqueur into each one.

"I practically never drink, but this is a special occasion," she said. "I'm going to make a toast."

"What's this dollar bill for?" I said.

"That's coming," she said. "The toast comes first."

"Listen to what's playing, Valerie." It was an old Stevie Wonder song coming through the Jensen speakers: "Ribbon in the Sky."

"That's nice," Valerie said.

"It could be our song."

"No, I don't want a song with you. I don't want

to do anything with you I ever did with someone before."

"Okay," I croaked out. I was really moved.

"Now, here's the toast," she said. "Hold your glass up."

My hand was shaking, too.

"Where love is," she said, "no room is too small. Say it, Henry."

"Where love is, no room is too small."

We clinked glasses and drank.

"Now," she said, "put down your glass."

It was a long while before we picked up the glasses again. The tape had stopped. The fog was thick around the windows of the car.

"If you don't let go of me," Valerie said, "I'm going to die of love."

"I'm already dead," I said.

Then I remembered the Dead of Winter Dance.

I sat up straight. "First I want to make a toast," I said, "and then I want to ask you something." I figured we could go to the dance late. Peter's stopped serving at ten. I could work out something with my brothers.

Valerie turned the tape over and picked up her glass.

I picked up mine.

"I Keep Forgettin' (Every Time You're Near)" was playing softly, and we were still looking into each other's eyes, in the candlelight.

"I still feel your breath on my cheek," I said, and I clinked my glass to hers.

She said, "Oh! Henry!"

"Well? Drink to it," I said softly.

She did, but she said again, "Oh, Henry! . . . What a beautiful thing to say. Oh, I wish you'd said it before I wrote what I did on the dollar."

"What did you write on the dollar?"

She picked up the dollar and ripped it in half.

"This half is yours," she said. "Can you see what it says?"

I held it up to the candle. " 'No room is too small,' " I read.

"Mine says, 'When two people are in love.' "

"Great," I said.

"You have to promise to keep your half as long as you love me, and to give it back when you don't love me anymore."

"I don't think you'll ever get this half back," I said.

"It's not as beautiful as what you said, though."

"It's beautiful, Valerie."

"What you said about my breath on your cheek is beautiful."

"This is beautiful, too, and the word 'love' is in it."

"Without a maybe anymore," she said.

"No more maybes," I said.

"No more maybes. . . . Oh, Henry."

"Oh, Valerie."

"What were you going to ask me?"

"I'm asking you to the Dead of Winter Dance," I said, "only we have to go a little late. Is that all right?"

"I wouldn't care what time we went if I could go with you."

"Good," I said.

"But I can't go with you, Henry."

"Why can't you go with me?"

"I'm going with Trevor Feldman."

"Trevor Feldman?"

"He asked me and I said I'd go."

"Valerie, what are you *talking* about?"

"Don't you remember, Henry? Daddy said I can't go out with you again until I go out with someone else first."

"Trevor Feldman?" My mind was whirling with the idea, and with the memory of Jody telling me she had private business to discuss with Trevor Feldman that noon in the cafeteria. Was that what she was discussing? Was that what she did with her life, run around from boy to boy feeding them little tidbits about Valerie's mood, Valerie's schedule, her thoughts and habits?

"Trevor's all right," Valerie said. "I don't love *him*."

"He comes up to your shoulder."

"Trevor says lots of famous men are short. Dudley

Moore, that movie star, is, and Mickey Rooney, Pablo Picasso was, and so was Yuri Gagarin."

"Who's he? Who's Yuri Gagarin?"

"He's the Soviet cosmonaut, Henry. Trevor says he was only five foot two. . . . Trevor's going to M.I.T."

"Valerie, how can you do this to me after I just said I still feel your breath on my cheek?"

"What do you want me to do, Henry?"

"Why do you have to go to the damn dance at all?"

"If I don't go on a date, I can't ever go on a date with you. I'm doing it for you, Henry."

"If you're doing it for me, why throw in that Trevor Feldman is going to M.I.T. What do I care where he goes to college?"

"That was just an aside, Henry."

"Some aside."

"You sound just like Daddy. That's what he'd say. Some aside."

"I don't want to sound just like Daddy, Valerie. I'm not really very fond of Daddy right this minute."

"He'll grow on you, Henry. And I hope you'll grow on him."

"Do you have a song with Trevor Feldman?"

"Of course I don't have a song with him. I don't really know him all that well. I really just met him at cheerleading practice."

"He's a cheerleader?"

"He's too little to be on any team."

92

"Trevor Feldman," I said.

"Henry?" she said. "We have to blow out the candles and go. It's ten minutes to eleven."

I just sat there glowering.

"Henry?" she said.

"What?"

She snuggled up against me for a moment. "Henry?"

"I *said* what?"

She ran her fingernail along my upper lip. "Him," she said, tapping her nails against my lips, "she loves. She really does."

"Well, him is damn mad!"

"I know him is," she said, sitting up and starting the car.

She dropped me off and I stormed into our upstairs, nearly knocking over an enormous vase of red roses on a table in the hall.

I could hear the eleven-o'clock TV news from the living room.

There was a card on the table beside the roses, and I picked it up and read it:

Marie, you mean so much to me.

Marie was my mother's first name.

"Is that you, Henry?"

"It's me, Mom."

"I was worrying about you, honey."

I walked into the living room. My brother Ernie

was asleep in the Barcalounger before the TV. My mother was sitting up on the couch in her white robe, with strips of gauze covering her face and neck.

"What happened to you? For God's sake, Mom, what—"

"Calm down," she said. "It's just a skin treatment."

"Do you have a disease?"

"I don't have anything. Old skin. Wrinkles."

She pointed to a book spread open on the table.

Circled in red on one page was "Mummified Face Wrap."

It began: "Cut three strips of two-inch-wide gauze to cover face . . ." and ended: ". . . your skin will have received deep moisturization and temporary tightening."

"What's all this about?" I said. "Why are you turning yourself into a mummy?"

"Not now, Henry," she said through the gauze. "It's hard for me to smile."

I turned the book over and read the title. *How to Look Ten Years Younger*.

"What's going on here?" I said.

Ernie groaned and shot the chair into a "sit" position.

"Do you have to wake up the whole house?" he asked me.

"Are you the whole house?"

"Sometimes I think I am. I thought you were coming back to help with the cleanup?"

"I didn't make it," I said.

"Next time when you don't make it, come in on tiptoe, Henry. Enter the house in a humble mood, next time you can't make it. Don't come barging in here like you were a breadwinner."

"I'm sorry," I said. "I'm just not used to having a mummy waiting up for me."

"Mummies always wait up for their little boys," Ernie said.

"And who sent the roses?"

"If you were ever around Peter's, you'd know. Mom's got herself a boyfriend."

"I *told* you it's hard for me to smile," Mom said.

"Who's your boyfriend?"

Ernie liked to do imitations.

" 'For a pearl of a car,' " he said, " 'try Earl T. Farr.' "

10

"If a famous movie star like Marilyn Monroe couldn't find happiness, that ought to tell you something." Earl T. Farr blew a smoke ring.

"What it ought to tell you," said Lena Bunch, "is that no one takes a beautiful woman seriously. Someday I intend to be a film director, and if I ever come upon a super-fantastic talent like Marilyn Monroe, she can play any part she wants!"

This conversation was at a table in Peter's. My mother was taking a break between songs. Lena, in Seaville for the weekend, was going to the Dead of Winter Dance, as my date, dressed as Marilyn Monroe. I had just changed out of my Peter's blazer and

96

come back downstairs in jeans, a work shirt, vest, boots, and a ten-gallon hat. I was going to the dance as James Dean, when he appeared in the old movie *Giant*.

"What it ought to tell you," Earl T. Farr persisted, "is that looks aren't everything. You yourself look very nice, Lena, and that's not my point, but—"

I tuned out.

All week Valerie had been describing things she was going to do to herself to look like Marilyn Monroe. (The only discussion I'd had with Lena about her costume was a short long-distance call—"I want to surprise you, Henry.")

"Sit down, Mr. James Dean. Ha! Ha! Join us!" said Earl T. Farr.

"I think Henry's eager to get to the dance," my mother said.

"I am," I said.

I was also eager to find out how my own mother could possibly see anything in Earl T. Farr. I'd finally remembered him from New Year's Eve, when he'd sat blowing smoke rings in her direction.

It was hard to forget him climbing out of an oyster shell on television.

He was much shorter than my mother, too. That fact sent panicky pictures to my mind of Valerie with Trevor Feldman.

"One thing we're not going to do is panic," Valerie'd said. "We're going to handle the situation like adults. You'll be at the dance with someone else and so will I, but we'll know we'd rather be with each other."

"Right," I'd agreed. "We'll be fine."

"You sure you don't feel anything about this Lena Bunch?"

"That's run its course," I'd said. "Are you sure you don't have a teeny-weeny little thing for Trevor Feldman?"

"*Nada,*" she'd said. "Zero. . . . This is going to be easy for us, Henry. It might even be fun."

"We'll make a game out of it!"

"Gawd, what kind of a name is Lena Bunch?" Valerie'd said.

"I suppose there's nothing funny about a name like Trevor Feldman?"

"Let's not start, Henry. We're starting to get panicky."

"There's nothing wrong with either name," I'd said. "They're fine names."

"Names aren't important anyway," Valerie'd said.

All week we'd get little fires like that started, then stamp them out before they raged.

I could feel a fire smoking deep inside me, as I drove along with Lena. I supposed Trevor Feldman drove something like a Porsche, possibly a Jaguar. . . . I knew he didn't have *Peter's Restaurant, Continental & German Cuisine—555-2598* on his car door.

It was a beautiful moonlit night, so bright you could see eye color.

As we drove toward Seaville High in the Jeep Wagoneer (Lena in white from head to toe) Lena talked about Alfred Hitchcock's films. I'd forgotten how Lena went over and over details of old movies.

". . . and then in *Spellbound*," she was saying, "which is my very favorite of all his films—in *Spellbound* . . .*"

Valerie, I was saying in my mind, *how did I know she'd come as Marilyn Monroe? Do you think I knew?*

". . . that single flash of color, remember, Henry? *Spellbound* was a black-and-white film except for that single flash of . . ."

What do you mean you bet your ass you knew? Wrong, Valerie! Wrong and unfair!

". . . color when the suicide shot the gun, that flash of . . ."

But if you were ever fair, Mars wouldn't be a planet and Trevor Feldman . . .

". . . red," Lena said.

And Trevor Feldman wouldn't be a . . . and Trevor Feldman . . .

"Henry, I don't think you're even listening."

"That single flash of red," I said. "I'm listening."

"You may be listening, Henry, but I don't think you're hearing."

"Lena, if I'm listening, I'm hearing. That's what listening means."

"Don't shout at me, Henry. . . . . It's the same old thing. If I talk about my career, what I intend to do with my life, you tune out."

"Lena," I said, "please. We're going to a dance. We're not planning our lives."

"Sometimes I wonder why you asked me to go to this dumb dance with you in the first place!"

"I asked you because you were going to be out here this weekend."

"And I accepted because I thought at least a little of the magic might be left. Just a little."

"You can't force magic, Lena."

"Then let's be friends, Henry. Just friends. Let's not try to be anything but friends."

"Fine," I said. "Fine. Friends."

The gym was jammed, and Ironing Bored was playing full force. While Lena went into the girls' room to comb her hair, Nelson Flower sidled up to me, his face, hair, and hands painted white. He had a sign around his neck that read: ANOTHER MAN FROM AMONG THE DEAD (Don't miss *Our Town*).

He was chewing on a Butterfinger. "Hi, Henry. Do you know what Piddle came as?"

"Is Valerie here?"

"Piddle came as Santa Claus. Santa Claus isn't supposed to be dead."

"Is Valerie here, Nelson?"

100

"She's dancing with Trevor Feldman. He's Napoleon."

"Where?"

"Somewhere out there." He waved the candy bar at the crowded floor.

He said, "Her sister's Judy Garland. She's here with Ronald Feldman, and he's John Lennon."

Lena came up behind me and purred, "I think I'm the only Marilyn Monroe."

"Don't count on it, Lena."

"Why do you always want to let the air out of my balloon?"

"I don't always want to," I said. "It's just a little too early to be so sure you're the only Marilyn Monroe."

It didn't take me long to find Valerie in the crowd. She had on a blond wig, and she was all in white, too. She looked like she was dancing all by herself until you looked down. Then you caught a glimpse of Trevor Feldman in a frock coat, knee breeches, boots, and a cocked hat.

"I could really just die!" Lena said when she spotted Valerie.

When Valerie saw us, she did a double take. Then she moved in closer to Trevor Feldman. She put her arms around him, smashing his nose into her neck.

"Lena," I said. "Don't let another Marilyn rattle

you. Let's really enjoy this dance." Valerie's fingers were playing with Trevor Feldman's hair.

"Thanks, Henry, for trying to make me feel better. That's a wig she has on. At least I'm a natural blond."

"Lena? Pretend it's the old days and we're Henry and Lena again."

Valerie was leaning down and cooing into Trevor Feldman's ear.

"Oh, Henry, what a nice thing to say."

"We're Henry and Lena," I said, "and we're—"

"Or we're Lena and Henry."

"Or we're Lena and Henry," I said, "and we're the Couple. Remember?" I was blowing into her ear.

"Some of the magic's coming back, isn't it, Henry?"

"Definitely," I told her. "It really is."

But magic of that sort didn't come back, and the heaviest thing in the world was a girl in your arms you used to go steady with.

While Ironing Bored took a break, I charged across to get some punch for Lena and me. I'd spotted Valerie to the right of the punch bowl, sitting in a folding chair beside Jody.

"Thanks a lot, Henry," Valerie said. "If you wanted to humiliate me, you found the way to do it."

"How did I know she'd come as Marilyn Monroe. Do you think I knew?"

"You bet your ass you knew!"

"What do you mean you bet your—"

102

"Break it up!" Jody said. "I'm just surprised there aren't more Marilyns around. There are three other Judys."

Valerie said to me, "You could have warned me."

"Hi, Jody," Jody said. "Happy sixteenth birthday!"

"I didn't find out until she walked into Peter's at nine o'clock!" I said.

"How was your Sweet Sixteen party, Jody?" Jody said.

Valerie said, "I don't really care, Henry. I really don't. . . . Trevor's been telling me about his plans to be an architect."

"Is he going to build little dollhouses?"

"Whatever he does, it won't be a poo, Henry."

Jody said, "Oh, it was a wonderful party, thank you, Henry. The Peking Buddha Delight was simply superb!"

Trevor came strolling up with his sword in his scabbard, carrying two glasses of punch, white gloves hanging through epaulets on his shoulder.

"Out of the way, Cowboy," he said.

His fifteen-year-old brother was right behind him, in love with himself, doing a little freestyle dancing while he sang "Imagine" and peered out through round wire glasses without lenses.

During the next set, Lena said, "Henry, you're holding me awfully hard."

I could see Valerie and Trevor Feldman sitting on the sidelines, holding hands.

I could hear "Out of the way, Cowboy," ringing in my ears.

Piddle danced by with our French teacher, who was dressed as Joan of Arc. Piddle hadn't had to stuff his Santa Claus costume. Out of the side of his mouth, as he passed me, he said, "Is dancing an appropriate expression for someone in your situation, Mr. Schiller?"

"What does that mean?" Lena asked me.

Valerie and Trevor were smiling raptly at each other.

"I'll explain later," I said. "How about more punch? I'll go get it."

"We just had punch."

"We need more."

"There's a lot about this night I don't understand," Lena said.

"Some nights are like that," I said, and I ran to get punch, and get in a few more snide remarks, none of them fazing Valerie one bit.

"Henry?" Lena finally said. "Should we go out to the car for a while? Would that help?"

We were barreling down the Montauk Highway half an hour later.

"I didn't mean that I wanted to leave the dance," she said.

I didn't say anything.

"At least at the dance we were beginning to feel like our old selves."

I just kept going.

"It was a mistake to suggest going out to the car," Lena said.

"It's not your fault," I said.

"It's not your fault, either, Henry. It was just too soon for all of that. We should have just kept dancing."

"Yeah."

"You're right. You can't force magic."

"No, you can't."

"You know how I always remember us, Henry? Not us now, but us then?"

"How?"

"Remember in *From Here to Eternity* when Burt Lancaster and Deborah Kerr made love on the beach?"

"We never made love on a beach, Lena."

"But if we ever had, we would have made love the way they did in *From Here to Eternity*."

"Lena, we're not in a movie. That's all."

"You're in one of your funny moods, Henry. I can tell something's coming."

"Seaville Cottages is coming," I said. "I'm dropping you off, Lena."

"Don't ever call me again, Henry," Lena said. "Don't ever write to me."

"You wrote to me," I said.

"You never got over the fact I threw that ring out the taxi window," she said.

"That ring cost me one hundred and sixty-five dollars," I said.

After I dropped Lena, I took off so fast the gravel in the driveway hit the fenders, and the tires squealed.

I headed back the way I'd come.

I can't say I had a plan, only a direction: Ocean Road.

11

Sometimes since my father's death, I had the feeling he was watching me. Usually I had it when I was doing something slightly crazy, like waiting for Valerie to come home that night, in the Kissenwisers' bushes.

It never stopped me, but it made me uncomfortable, because I suspected it made him uncomfortable, too: There was his youngest son, off his rocker, a little after midnight, crouching in the rhododendrons in a ten-gallon hat.

What was his son doing? Did he ask himself that? What had he done (or not done) to produce such a son, and what would become of this son?

What I was doing, as far as I knew, was waiting for Trevor Feldman's car to roll up the driveway. In my hand was my half of the dollar bill Valerie had given me. If Trevor Feldman tried anything in the car, or on the front porch, I was prepared to leap out of the bushes and return my half of the dollar.

That's your plan? I heard my father ask me. What if nothing happens?

If nothing happens, I told him, I walk back to my car down in the middle of Ocean Road, and go home. She doesn't even have to know I was there.

That was the conversation going on in my head, when I saw the lights of the car coming toward me.

"I just dropped by to return something," I intended to say.

If they started anything in the front seat of the car, I would knock on the window.

If it happened on the front step, I would grab Trevor by his sword and say, "I have something to return to Miss Monroe!"

If she led him inside, into the very hallway where we'd shared our first kiss, I'd come crashing through the front door.

Whatever happened had better happen fast. I'd had too many glasses of fruit punch and my bladder felt as though it would burst.

It was a long black car that stopped only a moment, while Valerie got out. The little yo-yo didn't even know enough to wait for her to get safely inside!

As the car pulled away, I popped out.

"Don't go inside yet, please!"

"Henry!"

"I had to come here, Valerie. I had to—"

"Oh, Henry, I'm so glad to see you! But Daddy's going to just kill you! He's putting the car in the garage."

"What happened to Trevor?"

"Daddy drove us. Trevor's family needed their car tonight. Jody and Daddy will be here any second, Henry! Henry, I didn't mean anything I said."

"I didn't mean anything *I* said."

"What are we going to do? Daddy's—"

"I'll just go."

"Don't go! Hurry, Henry." She was pulling me through the front door.

She said, "I'll hide you until you can slip out later."

"Where will you hide me?"

"Not down here. Daddy and Jody are going to make cocoa."

We were on our way up the front stairs. Valerie had her fingers to her lips. "Quietly," she whispered. "Mother and Gran are asleep."

When we got inside her room, she shut the door and leaned against it, laughing hard with her hands to her mouth.

"Lock it!" I whispered. "Lock the door!"

She could hardly get words out she was laughing so hard. "Da-daddy duh-doesn't be-lieve in locks."

Valerie's room was all pink and white, with a queen-sized canopy bed in its center. The wallpaper was pink roses on a white background, and the bedspread and a chaise longue were in the same pattern. There were framed photographs everywhere, as though all the eyes of her family were fixed on me. Mrs. Trump smiled up from a croquet game on the bureau, and Mrs. Kissenwiser looked pensive in her garden. Jody's braces flashed in the sun in a scene with Valerie on a boat. Al Kiss was everywhere, in front of microphones, on stages with dancing girls behind him, in darkened nightclubs, in bear hugs with Merv Griffin, Milton Berle, Alan King, etc., and in white tails with a white carnation in his buttonhole, with "To my own dear daughter, Valley," scrawled across it, "from your loving poppy!"

"Oh, Henry, this is wild!" Valerie said, tossing her coat across her bed. "Oh, honey"—coming toward me—"this is off-the-wall won-der-ful!"

"You're not mad?"

"Mad? I love intensity. I love it that you were driven to come here! What happened to your date? You ditched her, *didn't* you, Henry?"

She had ahold of my jeans' belt.

"Valerie, I have to go."

"Where do you think you're going to go with Daddy right downstairs?"

"No. I mean, I have to *go.*"

"Oh! Well, go. My bathroom's right in there."

110

I started in the direction she pointed. "What if he comes up here?"

"He always knocks," she said.

"But what if he wants to come in?"

"I'll han-dle it, Henry!" She was laughing again. "And take off that hat!" she called after me. "I feel like a rodeo groupie."

When I came out of the bathroom, Valerie was waiting for me just outside the door. So was Nachus. Valerie'd turned on her television, and I caught a glimpse of Charlton Heston dressed as Moses, in the old movie *The Ten Commandments*, before she began kissing me.

"One thing," she was whispering into my mouth, as she planted little kisses all around my lips, "I love . . . about this . . . is that . . . it's so . . . sort of . . . il-legal," and she giggled.

"One thing," I followed suit, "I love . . . about this . . . is that . . . we're in . . . your . . . bed . . . room."

"Oh, Henry, I had a dismal time with Trevor Feld-man."

Kiss. Kiss. Kiss.

"I hated my whole evening," I whispered.

"I imagined you kissing her. Did you kiss her?"

"You're the only one I kiss."

Kiss. Kiss. Kiss.

Nachus was cleaning herself vigorously, as though she was being contaminated.

"Henry?"

"What?"

Kiss. Kiss.

"I love you. I loved you ever since you smiled at me and said we can do fish, we can do lobster, we can do—"

"Frogs' legs," I whispered. "I love you, Valerie."

"I love you."

"I loved you ever since you came through the front door with the snow melting in your hair."

"I loved you ever since you said we have room in the back for parties."

"I loved you before I met you," I whispered. "I was waiting for you."

She stood on tiptoe and kissed my forehead. "I loved you before I was born," she said. She kissed my right ear, and then my left ear. "I love your ears. I love the fact you can play Ping-Pong without a paddle."

"I love you," I said.

"I love you more."

"I love the fact you have a body that won't quit," I said. "It won't even take a lunch break."

"It will with you."

From the TV, Moses said, "After this day, you shall see his chariots no more!"

There was a loud knock on the door.

"Valley, honey?" Al Kiss said. "I brought you up some cocoa."

12

"Valley, honey, I'm not going to stay. I just want you to have some cocoa."

"Daddy, I told you I don't want any cocoa."

"I'm just going to put it over here. It's Droste, honey. It's good stuff."

"I can't believe you barged in here when I said I didn't want any cocoa and I'm dead tired."

"This will pick you up."

"I don't want to be picked up. I want to go to sleep."

I could hear it all from behind the shower curtain, in Valerie's pink tub. The shower curtain was the same pink-roses-on-a-white-background pattern as the wallpaper in her room, the bedspread, and the chaise. There was a pink plastic razor in a pink soap dish, along with a bar of pink soap in the shape of a rose.

"Hey, honey, is someone's nose a little out of joint, hah? You could have had a Sweet Sixteen party but you didn't want one. Remember I wanted to make you one at the Plaza?"

"Daddy, Jody's Sweet Sixteen party didn't bother me a bit. *Please*."

"Then what's going on? How come you're making a beeline for your room and not having cocoa?"

I heard bedsprings.

Was he sitting down?

"You can't sit down, Daddy. I'm really, honestly, super-tired."

"I'm not going to stay, honey. I'm just trying to find out what's wrong. Pass me that saucer under the cup. I need an ashtray."

I got a whiff of his cigar.

"Daddy, please don't smoke. I'll get a headache."

"Since when? You're the one that loves cigar smoke. That's what you always tell your mother when she's on my back about it. What's wrong with you tonight? Did Trevor Feldman try any funny business?"

"I don't want to talk about Trevor Feldman."

"Are you mad at me because I want you to date around?"

"I'm not mad at you. But I'm going to get mad at

114

you if I can't just crawl into bed and get some sleep."

"Go in the bathroom and put on your nightie, hon. I'll tuck you in."

"I'll talk to you tomorrow, Daddy. That cigar smoke is—"

Nachus was on her hind legs, peering into the tub.

"It's out, honey. See? Cigar's out. Get yourself ready for bed and I'll tuck you in."

"You have to go, Daddy. I don't feel like talking."

"Then may I say something, pussums?"

Nachus looked about ready to leap into the tub. I gave her nose a push.

"Can't you say it tomorrow?"

"I'm leaving early tomorrow morning, lovey."

"I'll get up and have breakfast with you."

"And I'll turn into the Pope."

"I will, Daddy. I want to get up early tomorrow."

"Why? What's getting you out of bed before noon on a Sunday? What's so important you're going to get up at the crack of dawn?"

"I'll have breakfast with you before you go."

Nachus' dark-brown nose made another appearance around the shower curtain.

"Please. I don't want any such shock so early in the morning. I just have this to say to you, lambie-kins. I'm not a heavy. You know I'm not a heavy. If I thought that Heinrich was going to count in your life, I'd figure out a way to accommodate the idea,

115

but I don't want all this *tsuris* for that nebbish."

"He's not a nebbish, Daddy, and I don't want to talk about it."

The blue cross-eyes of Nachus were studying me.

"Get ready for bed, then. You're not going to sleep in that dress, are you? I wouldn't be surprised if Marilyn Monroe slept in hers. I met her once in this little club outside Philadelphia, and she wasn't so together upstairs, you know what I mean? She had this little voice." He was actually trying to do an imitation of her. " 'Oh, Mr. Kiss, I think your jokes shocked some of the Quakers in the audience. We're in Quaker country, Mr. Kiss.' . . . I said don't worry about it, Marilyn. Some of my best Jews are Friends!"

"Daddy." This weak-sounding little voice from Valerie. A long sigh.

Nachus had jumped into the tub, and was smelling my boots and making a face.

"I just want to tell you the last thing I'd do is forbid you anything, sweetheart, particularly when it comes to romance. You don't know the hell your grandmother put me through when I fell in love with your mother. She was ready to bell me like some leper so the whole family'd be warned if I came anywhere near the house. I think she'd still like to bell me. So don't tell me I don't know what it's like to be in love and have obstacles thrown in your path instead of rosebuds. The whole world doesn't love a lover if it's a world that includes Ida Trump, and you ought to know that."

"Then you understand?" Valerie said. . . . Then he understands? I asked the pink-and-white tiles I was resting my head against. He understands? I asked Nachus.

"Of course I understand. I understand *love*, Valley. I was so in love with your mother, you wouldn't think so now, maybe, but your grandmother'd put her on a train, I'd meet the train, put her on a plane to get her away from me, I'd meet the plane. I spent all my time at train stations, bus depots, airports, waiting to meet your mother who was getting sent off to never see me again."

"Okay. You understand. Good night, Daddy."

"Your mother and I may not be that loving anymore, the fires die down, but Romeo and Juliet couldn't hold a candle to us in our day."

"I'm glad you understand, Daddy, but I'm getting a headache."

"Since when? You with a headache? You never had a headache in your life."

"I'm getting my first one."

Nachus jumped back out of the tub.

"See, Valley, all that love stuff, all you go through, it's worth it. I'm the first one to tell you it's worth it. But not for some nebbish. I don't want you spending your emotion for some—"

"Say it, Daddy. I know what you're going to say."

"Nebbish. I said it already."

"That's not what you were going to say."

"What was I going to say?"

"You know what you were going to say."

What was he going to say?

"I wasn't going to say that," Al Kiss said. Say what? "I just don't see what you see in him."

"He has a great face. Okay?"

"Hitler had a great face, too."

"I knew something like that was coming."

"I take it back. Hitler's face wasn't so great."

"Daddy, he's not even a real German."

"He's German. He's got Deutschland written all over his puss, honey. I hear *'Deutschland über Alles'* coming out of his brain on a secret wavelength, and I smell sauerkraut oozing out of his pores, and I see swastikas in his eyes. He's Boche, honeybunch."

"I don't want to talk about it, Daddy. You're too bigoted."

"Bigoted? *Me?* Oh, Valley, you've got to take that back or I'm going to sleep at the foot of your bed like a dog tonight. Valley, no one's ever called Al Kiss bigoted."

" 'He's got Deutschland written all over his puss'? . . . What would you call that?"

"I'm just talking informally here, pussums, father to daughter, and you know it. I don't even care that he's German. You know that? We've got German

118

blood, too. You know that?"

"Then why are you carrying on so about it? Why can't you let me sleep?"

"Get into your nightie. Go change and we'll talk while you're changing. I don't want hard feelings between us because I get in a few knocks at Heinrich. I don't like you to say seriously that I'm bigoted."

"Okay. You're not bigoted. Okay?"

"I'm not, Valleykins."

Nachus was sitting on the floor of the bathroom, watching me through the shower curtain.

"I said you're not."

"I don't want you saying it just to get rid of me."

"Spend the night at the foot of my bed, then, but let me get some sleep."

He was probably getting down on the rug and curling up.

"It doesn't matter to me if you date Italians, Frenchmen, Germans—just don't *fall* for someone who's so completely not from us. There. Okay? That's what I'm talking."

"Just don't date a goy. Just don't mess with a *shaygets*," she said. "I knew you'd get around to saying it."

"I said just don't *fall* for one. Save yourself that heartbreak."

"We're not even that religious, Daddy."

"We're one heart, honey. We're a people of one heart. It's in here."

119

Nachus was watching me carefully.

I shifted my weight from my left foot to my right. I let out a little stored-up breath in a slow, silent stream, and let some air quietly in through my nose.

"Daddy, I really do have a headache."

"I'm on my feet. I'll just say something else about this kid."

"Please don't."

Go right ahead. I'd like to hear it.

"His father—"

"Daddy! Don't go on and on!"

Go on and on. His father what? His *father*? He didn't even know my father. *I* hardly knew my father.

"His father got himself shot. He's got no father, Valley, to tell him what's what in life. He's got a restaurant is what he's got. My father, may he rest in peace, was the knight in shining armor I'd be nothing without today! How does a boy grow up and *be* someone without a father?"

I felt like weeping.

Al Kiss said, "I'm going. I'm going. Don't make motions. But let me tell you, sweetheart, I'd hate to be a young man with no father. It's nowhere. Poor as we were, I grew up rich. I had my father's philosophy! I had books! I had Maimonides! Heinrich's got a recipe for sausage and red cabbage! Do you see what I mean? How's he going to know how to treat you? Where's his example? Who's going to point out poos to him, hah? Hey, you're pushing me!"

"I have a raging headache, Daddy!"

"I'll get you an aspirin."

"NO!"

"What's the matter, I can't get you an aspirin?" and he was on the other side of the shower curtain suddenly, starting to rattle the bottles inside the bathroom cabinet above the sink.

Then suddenly there was S I L E N C E.

"What the hell is the seat doing up in here?" he said.

S i l e n c e.

"Whose cowboy hat is this?" he said. "And what's Nachus looking at?"

Nachus let out a long hiss over her shoulder.

Al Kiss flung back the shower curtain.

"ACH-CHOO!" all over me. "ACH-CHOO!"

13

"Henry? This is Valerie."

"Valerie? This is Henry. What's this Henry-this-is-Valerie garbage, Valerie? I love you. I knew you'd have a bedroom like that. Is everything all right? Where are you?"

"Henry, I called to tell you that I don't want anything to do with you anymore."

"Ah, you're home. You're home and he's telling you to say that."

"This is my own decision, Henry."

"Then why do you sound like a robot, Valerie?"

"Please don't call here or come here."

"You think I want to come there and have my arm

pulled out of my socket again? He pulled my arm out of my socket!"

"Please don't make it hard for me in school."

"Please don't come to school with your long black hair falling down your back smelling of summer flowers."

"Because I really mean what I've just said, Henry."

"You don't mean what you've just said. What about when two people are in love, no room is too small?"

"Good-bye, Henry," she said. "Forever."

At quarter to eight Monday morning in a blinding snowstorm out behind Seaville High, I said, "Valerie? Wait! *Wait!*"

"She can't talk to you, Henry," Jody said through a mouth slit in her parka.

"I'll talk to him," Valerie said, white wet snowflakes on a soft field of long black hair. "Can we go inside for this little discussion?"

"You're not supposed to talk to him," Jody said.

"What kind of psychoanalyst do you think you're going to be?" I asked Jody. "You have no human emotions."

I was tagging behind them, icicles about to form on my ears.

"I don't want to be a shrink anymore," Jody said. "It depresses me to think about human emotions. I prefer computers with artificial intelligence."

"Hey!" I said. "Hold the door open for me! It's

Monday morning. I'm pregnant."

But it didn't even get a smile from Valerie.

I squeezed inside the entranceway after them, and Valerie told Jody to go on, she'd handle it.

"I love you," I said.

She shut her eyes as though she was in pain, then opened them and looked right into mine. "I promised my father, Henry."

"I know that. I knew that Sunday morning when you made that stupid 'Henry, this is Valerie' call."

"I've never broken a promise I made to him."

"What did you make a promise like that for? You can't keep that promise."

"I had a long talk with him, Henry. We can't see each other anymore."

"Whose idea was it to drag me up to your bedroom?"

"It was all my fault. I told him that."

"What did you tell him that for? You knew he'd go bananas if you told him it was your idea to drag me up to your bedroom!"

"I can't lie to my father, Henry. You don't know how it is."

"That's right. You've got a father you can't lie to and I've got a recipe for sausage and red cabbage!"

"I'm sorry, Henry. We were getting in too deep."

"We didn't even get in, for Pete's sake. We didn't even—"

She was heading down the hall, away from me.

124

So it went that last week of January and into February.

Valerie even made a suggestion to Mr. Piccara that the leads in the school play practice without the minor characters present.

In a desperate attempt to foil this plan, I called her house while she was at aerobic dancing.

Mrs. Kissenwiser answered the phone.

"I'm calling for Mr. Piccara," I said, on the afternoon of a night the minor characters were going through the script. "We need Valerie at rehearsal tonight."

"The rehearsal of what?" Mrs. Kissenwiser said.

"The rehearsal of *Our Town*," I said. "The play Valerie's going to be in."

"I don't know anything about a play," Mrs. Kissenwiser said.

"She told you about a hundred times that she's playing Emily in *Our Town*," I said.

"This is you, isn't it?" she said. "You're not supposed to call here. My husband doesn't want you calling here or coming here."

Noontimes, Valerie was back running off to McDonald's in her car with the senior crowd. Jody was hanging out with Ronald Feldman in the cafeteria.

I'd get glimpses of Valerie, laughing down at Trevor Feldman in the halls between classes, giving a ride to Alan Gould or Perry Miller, once to Nelson

Flower, who I cornered in the hall next day.

"Did she mention me?"

"Not a word about you," he said. "You'd better come prepared to Piddle's class next time. He's really sore at you for not knowing what Lamaze training is."

"What did she talk about?" I asked him.

"She said she was applying to all these colleges, but she hoped she'd get into Antioch," he said. "My mother has a book called *Your Baby, Your Body: Fitness During Pregnancy,* if you want to borrow it."

"Where's Antioch?" I said. "Is Antioch near here?"

Near Valentine's Day, Fred gave me three dollars and said, "Get a valentine for Mom from me, and one for Angel."

I got him a big oversized mushy one for Mom, and I actually found one with an angel on it.

"Who's this one with the angel on it for?" he said.

"It's for Angel. Who did you think it was for?"

"What's she going to think if I give her one with an angel on it?" he said. "I haven't given her one with an angel on it for a long time. She's going to read something into it. She's going to think I've been playing around. I don't want to send her one with an angel on it after all this time, Henry. Can't you get me a plain old valentine, the to-my-wife kind?"

I sent the one with the angel on it to Lena, and wrote "Just for old times' sake, your friend, Henry," on the inside.

126

On Valentine's Day, I borrowed against my salary and bought a dozen red roses, which I left on the seat of Valerie's car. I wrote on the card: *I* still *feel your breath on my cheek! Love, Henry.*

"Henry," she said when I answered the phone that night. "You're not making it easy for me."

"I love you," I said.

Pause.

I said, "Did you get the roses?"

She laughed. "Trevor sat on them. A thorn went right through his pants. . . . Oh, Henry."

"Don't 'Oh, Henry' me," I told her. "What is this? We're in love and we don't even talk!"

"I heard that song on the radio today," she said.

"What song?"

"Remember when we were toasting each other down on the beach? 'The One That You Love' played. Remember? It broke my heart, Henry."

"I thought you didn't want to have a song."

"I don't want to have a song. Particularly now."

"Now is when we need one," I said. "Where are you?"

"I've dragged the phone into my bathroom, Henry. Every time I'm in here, I think of you."

"That's really romantic, Valerie. Is that the only place you think of me. The bathroom?"

"You know better than that."

"Why didn't you send me a valentine?"

"I promised Daddy, Henry. You know I made him a promise."

"Then what are you calling for?"

"I wanted you to know you're a thorn in Trevor Feldman's *tochis.* . . . Hey, Henry?"

"What?"

Long pause.

"Valerie? Are you still there?"

"I'm here. I'm looking at my tub. Remember my tub?"

"I love you," I said. "I love your tub and your pink plastic razor and your soap in the shape of a rose and—"

"Don't, Henry. This is cruel."

"Then what are you calling for?"

"I couldn't help myself," she said, "and I wanted to tell you Daddy's on the NBC Valentine special tonight."

Click.

Behind me, Ernie said, "Henry, there's five schnitzel orders getting cold for table nine. Do you care?"

"You've got flour on your nose," I said. "You're getting flour on the Linzer tortes."

"Take the schnitzel to table nine," he said. "Then come back and get Mom's orchid out of the refrigerator. Earl wants you to present it to her right before she does her first number."

"Why doesn't Earl present it to her?"

"He won't get here until after midnight. He wants her to have it for Valentine's Day."

At ten o'clock, I told Fred to put on NBC, while I went by the bar with a tray of assorted tortes and coffee.

In the dining room, customers were singing with the oompah band:

> *Ist das nicht ein Hin und Her?*
> *Ja, das ist ein Hin und Her!*
> *Ist das nicht ein Lichtputzscher'?*
> *Ja, das ist ein . . .*

A party of eight arrived and ordered apple pancakes.

I was running around with trays, sneaking into the bar to catch glimpses of the TV, rushing to the cash register with money and checks.

Finally, Fred got my eye just as I was passing with the eight apple pancake orders.

"He's on, Henry."

I could hear Al Kiss's voice, but not what he was saying. I could hear laughter and applause, as I slid the eight plates off the tray, skidding around the table, then back out to the bar.

". . . So I put my foot down," Al Kiss was saying. "I said I don't want him around anymore. He's not to come here anymore. He's a mental case! . . . Well,

my mother-in-law—she's eighty-two, God bless her—
my mother-in-law looks up from the table at me and
she says, I know what a mantelpiece is, but what's a
mantelcase?"

Laughter.

"He's going at you tonight, Henry," Fred said. He
told a customer at the bar. "He's talking about
him,"—pointing at me.

Al Kiss said, "Ah, but don't get me wrong. I don't
have anything against Germans. I find their language
fascinating. I remember once before I told him to get
lost—I remember sitting out in our garden, Heinrich
and me and my daughter, and a butterfly goes by. My
daughter says the word 'butterfly' in English is said
to be one of the most beautiful words in any language.
She's poetic, my daughter. She said, Just listen:
but-ter-fly. It's beautiful. . . . And I said, Well, it's
not bad in Spanish, either. Mariposa. Just listen:
mar-ri-*pos*-sa. It's beautiful. . . . My daughter said,
And it's lovely in French, too. Papillon. Just listen:
pa-pee-*yawn*. Isn't it lovely? . . . I said, Well, it's
got a sweet sound in Italian, too. Farfalla. Just listen:
far-*fal*-la. . . . And this was when Heinrich spoke
up. Heinrich says, So what's wrong with Schmet-
terling?"

Laughter.

"Sch-met-ter-ling!" Al Kiss roared. "*Him* she
loves?"

The studio orchestra played while he threw kisses at the audience and bowed his way offstage.

The customer at the bar turned around on his stool and looked me over. "Yeah," he said, "you got a pair of ears on you."

"He did a whole bit on your ears when he came on," Fred said.

The customer said, "He called you Sauerkraut Breath."

I charged into the kitchen and dialed Valerie's number.

"Henry, don't get on the phone now," Ernie said. "You've got to serve coffee to the apple pancakes."

The phone rang once, twice.

"You forgot Mom's orchid, too," Ernie said.

"Mom hasn't gone on yet. They were playing *'Schnitzelbank.'* Didn't you hear everyone singing?"

"Mom's going on any minute," Ernie said.

Mrs. Trump said, "Hello?"

"I'd like to talk to Valerie, please."

"From The Restaurant?" Mrs. Trump said. "Is that you?"

"From The Restaurant. Heinrich. Mental Case. Sauerkraut Breath. Yes. It's me. I'd like to talk to Valerie, please, Mrs. Trump."

"Hoo-ha! You got some nerve saying what you'd like at forty-five minutes before midnight and she's got school tomorrow."

"I've got school tomorrow, too."

"Talk at school, not in the middle of the night. We go to bed around here."

"Mrs. Trump," I said, "I know you just watched him on TV. I know you're not asleep."

"You're putting me to sleep." She actually snored into the mouthpiece. "There. I'm asleep."

Click.

"Henry, the apple pancakes need their coffee! *Now!*"

When I went back into the dining room, Earl T. Farr was coming through the front door in a fur-collared coat, with a cigarette in a long holder in his mouth.

He caught ahold of my jacket. "Why doesn't she have on her orchid?" he asked me.

My mother gave a signal to the piano player.

"My fun-ny Val-en-tine," she began.

14

Two weeks later, I walked in the door one day after school, and found my mother with her head wrapped in a towel, Coty Sweet Earth smeared on her face in a lavender mask.

"Shhhh!" she said. "Look!" pointing at the TV.

Al Kiss was on.

"Now apparently I was wrong about Heinrich," he was saying. "He appears to be the missing link between anthropoid apes and human beings."

Laughter.

I sat down on the edge of the couch.

"My wife and I recently visited this restaurant his family runs. It's one of those *gemütlich* places where knobby-kneed fellows in short pants toot out *'Schnitzelbank'* and everyone sings in a haze of weinkraut and cigar smoke, while a stuffed moose stares down at you from the wall. . . . You know the kind of place? Knackwurst and bratwurst and you say to the waiter: This wall is so thin you can almost see through it. He says, That's the window you're looking at."

Laughter.

My mother was shaking her head from side to side.

"My wife actually heard this. She was on her way to the little girls' room and she passes Heinrich, who's on the telephone. Now, he's trying to get the number for Zabar's. What do I know? Maybe they're out of herring, maybe. . . . Maybe pumpernickel. Zabar's is this high-class deli in New York, and Heinrich's trying to get their number. My wife's going by and she hears Heinrich telling the operator: I want Zabar's! *Z! Z!* No, not *C! Z!* . . . A B C D E F G H I J K L M N O P Q R S T U V W X Y . . . *Z!* . . . *Him* she loves?"

On top of the television there was a new gold picture frame with a photograph of Earl T. Farr inside. It was one of those goony poses where the subject decides to squat down with one hand touching the ground, as though any moment a gun would go off and begin a race. He had a carnation in his buttonhole, and he was surrounded by used Fords.

"What can I tell you?" Al Kiss went on. "This

throw rug my daughter's made into wall-to-wall carpeting actually prepares some of the food they serve in that restaurant. He's a klutz, you know? He comes out of the kitchen to wait table with mashed potato in his hair. . . . Hey, Heinrich, I tell him, you got mashed potato in your hair. So he puts his fingers up and feels his hair. Feels the mashed potato. Then he looks at me and says, Jeez, I thought it was creamed spinach."

Laughter.

"*Him* she loves?"

My mother said, "Now he's picking on Peter's."

"He's not saying it's Peter's."

"Everyone will know it's Peter's," she said. "Why is he doing this?"

Merv Griffin asked Al Kiss the same question.

MERV: *You've really got a dynamite new act, Al. . . . Tell me something, this is a new Al Kiss, hmmm?*

AL KISS: Nu? *(Puff on the cigar as he gets it going.)*

MERV: *You know what I mean. I mean, there was never anything really personal in your act before, except about the gambling. You were the two-guys-meet-in-Las-Vegas type joke teller. We never heard anything about your family. Why this new flavor to your act? I really like it, but I'm curious.*

135

AL KISS:	*(Puff puff) I got a daughter in love. They say love is blind, but she sees twice as much in this* shlepper *as anyone else does.*
MERV:	*So this whole new thing came about when your daughter fell in love with this Heinrich? This isn't some gag writer's way of updating your act for the younger generation?*
AL KISS:	*This is true. No writer could make up Heinrich.*
MERV:	*It's been a great success, hasn't it? I mean, I see you all over the place lately. You're having a renaissance. This Heinrich has really given you something.*
AL KISS:	*You could say that. He's given me ulcers, insomnia, nightmares, dyspepsia.*
MERV:	*Well, we all wish you continued success, Al. I think you're lucky Heinrich came along.*
AL KISS:	*Some lucky!*

"Henry," my mother said after Al Kiss walked off to applause, "he's making a mountain out of a molehill, isn't he?"

"Now I'm a molehill," I said.

"You're not a molehill, but you hardly see this girl. Am I right?"

"I love her. If you weren't so busy trying to look younger for Earl T. Farr, you might begin to perceive

136

that I am in love with the daughter of Al Kiss."

"Leave Earl out of this, Henry. I'm asking you how often you see this girl. I thought you weren't seeing her anymore."

"I'm trying to see her."

"Oh, Henry, don't make yourself into a doormat just because she's some big star's daughter."

"When she came through our front door, I didn't know she was some big star's daughter. I fell in love with her on the spot."

"The day you don't fall in love on the spot is the day I'll sit up and listen. You fell in love with Kelly on the spot, Lena on the spot—"

"I fall in love on the spot. That's the way I am. But this time is different. Mom, you should *see* her!"

"I'd like to see her."

"You'll see her."

"When?"

"I'm working on it."

"Henry? Work on your schoolwork. You don't even mention your schoolwork. How are you doing in school?" Then she grinned and the lavender face mask cracked. "How pregnant are you now, Henry?"

"I'll be going into the third trimester soon," I said. "The fetal movements are getting stronger." I'd borrowed *Your Baby, Your Body: Fitness During Pregnancy* from Nelson Flower. "I'm going to have my baby at home, the Lamaze way: no anesthesia, no surgery, no stitches."

"Take a lot of iron," my mother said, "and get a lot of exercise. And stop worrying about Earl."

"I don't worry about Earl."

"Why don't you like him, Henry?"

"Because he crawls out of an oyster shell on television. What would Dad think of you dating some guy who crawls out of an oyster shell on the tube?"

"Your dad wasn't a jealous man. If he was looking down from heaven right now, what he'd be most worried about was that we only did sixty-one dinners last night."

At Seaville High, word had spread that I was Heinrich, and kids were shouting after me, "*Him* she loves?"

I was beginning to become a minor celebrity at school. Mornings, Marilyn Klaich, whose locker was next to mine, began initiating conversations with me. Annette Gould, who sat in front of me in French class, began turning around to borrow paper from me. Frosty Ward, captain of the girls' hockey team, told me to come along with her gang to Dirty Dottie's. Ernest Leogrande and Jonathan Karpinski, Seaville High's baseball stars, talked to me about going out for the team. When I entered the school cafeteria noons, half a dozen kids invited me to their tables.

I decided to take a new tack with Valerie. No more trying to corner her out in the parking lot. No more passing Jody notes for her. I sneaked glimpses of her without her knowing it, every one a stab to my insides

138

that I bore in silence. I even told Nelson Flower not to tell me a single thing she said those times she gave him a ride to the corner of Main Street and Maritime Lane.

"But she's started to ask about you," he said.

"Who cares?" I answered. "What, in particular, did she ask about?"

"She asked if Piddle was still on your case."

"Let her ask," I said. "Did she ask anything else?"

"She said she heard you went to Dirty Dottie's with Frosty."

"I don't even want to hear about it," I said.

"She said she misses you."

"She said that?"

"That's what she said. She said, 'I miss him, Nelson.' "

"Never mind," I said, my heart racing away.

"Next time I'll tell her you don't want to hear a single thing she says," Nelson said. "I'll probably be out a ride after that. I think she only gives me a ride so she can talk about you, and then have me tell you what she said."

"Then don't tell her I said I don't want to hear a single thing she said. Just don't come and tell me anything she said, unless you think it's important."

I held out my hand for some M&M's he passed me from his package and we walked along silently for a while. I said, "Even if it isn't important you can tell me, I guess."

"I don't ever want to fall in love," he said. "It's the pits."

Weeks passed.

One night after the whole cast rehearsed *Our Town*, I was walking down Main Street with Nelson when her car pulled up. She rolled down the window and said, "Who needs a ride?"

My phantom self dashed toward the car, flung open the door, pulled her from behind the steering wheel, and kissed her until my lips hurt.

My real self just shrugged and walked along weak kneed and breathless.

"Go ahead," Nelson told me.

"You go ahead."

"I don't need a ride. I'm almost home."

I called out, "Thanks but no thanks!"

The white convertible went on.

"Here," Nelson said, passing me half of his 3 Musketeers bar. "You probably need some sugar now."

The next day, Jody was waiting for me outside the cafeteria. I stepped away from Ernest Leogrande and Jonathan Karpinski to talk to her when she crooked her finger at me.

"Okay. She's going crazy. Okay?" Jody said.

"People are like onions," I said. "You have to peel back layer after layer."

"Hello, Henry."

"Hello, Jody."

140

"I'm not supposed to fraternize with you, either, but I'm fraternizing with you just long enough to tell you Val's going crazy and she wants to see you."

"Oh," I said, " a command performance."

"Something like that."

"Thrill thrill," I said.

"You don't care, though, do you?"

"Why should I care?" I said. "All of that was a long time ago."

"Why are little beads of sweat forming on your upper lip?" she said.

"It must be all this fraternization," I said.

"If you don't care . . ." She shrugged and started into the cafeteria.

"I CARE!"

"Okay," she said. "Okay. Don't blow a gasket."

"Why doesn't she just come up to me and tell me she wants to see me?"

"She doesn't want Trevor to know. The Feldmans are friends of the family. My mother and Mrs. Feldman are like that." She crossed two fingers together.

Then she took a tiny bottle of Binaca Breath Drops out of her jacket pocket, unscrewed the top, and touched the bottle to her lips.

"What are you doing that for?"

"Because Val said I should whisper this to you. I don't want to offend."

She smelled strongly of mint as she got on tiptoe and whispered into my right ear: "She says to wait outside Nelson Flower's house after school today. Got it?"

"Henry," she said, "oh, Henry," she said, "dearest," she said, "the one I loved before you were even born, you've got to think of something!"

We were racing toward the dunes under a cold winter sky so blue and white and sunny the beauty of it hurt. Her beauty hurt. Her long, soft black hair and light-green eyes hurt, and I sat so close to her I had a fleeting memory of myself when I was tiny and didn't yet know about the pain girls could inflict on your soul, and sat between my father's legs while he steered an old car we had.

"You've got to think of something!" she went on. "I'm dying on the vine, Henry! I want you to love me. Only you, Henry."

"I've got to think of something," I said. "I want to be ground up with the meat for the Königsberger klops, and thrown out with the sauerkraut water if I can't have you! How come he calls me Sauerkraut Breath? Do I have sauerkraut breath?"

"You have the sweetest breath that ever breathed on me. He just goes for the laughs. . . . Oh, Henry!"

She was steering with one hand, the other hand holding on to mine for dear life.

"I don't care if we die!" I said, a little concerned about her driving.

"I hope we do!" she said.

142

"I'd just as soon not," I said.

"We have to stop this car very soon," she said.

"Don't go over the dunes."

"I believe we could fly. The two of us could fly, Henry."

"Not in the car," I said. "Stop the car or we'll drown. Why do you always smell like summer flowers or vanilla cookies?"

"Why are your eyes so brown? Why did I die a million deaths every day we were apart?"

"Don't talk so much about dying," I said. "Wait until we're parked."

She pulled off the road, an inch away from a dune.

She turned off the key to stop the motor, turned it back on to keep the power, cranked up the emergency brake, and shoved in a tape.

Music flooded the car, some old Elton John tune. She had her mouth on mine, kissing me, talking the words being sung.

Then she was holding me with one arm, and pushing down the door handle with her other hand. "Henry, I need to be all wrapped around you!"

"Where? . . . The dunes!" It was about twenty-eight degrees, with a saltwater wind so fast and cold sea gulls were shivering on the telephone lines above us.

She jumped out of the car. "You have to think of something because this sort of thing can't continue!"

I got out of the car, too, my ears ringing in the icy

143

gale. "No, it can't continue."

"I want to love you, Henry!"

"Yes. Pick a spot." I imagined us hours later frozen somewhere on the ocean sands into a solid block.

But she was pushing back the front seat of the car, crawling into the backseat.

"Hurry, Henry!"

15

So winter went into spring, with Valerie and me secret lovers, suspected by half of Seaville High and all the adult Kissenwisers. Valerie was questioned daily ("grilled" was her description of it) by her father, when he was home, her mother, and Mrs. Trump: Where did you go after school? and who were you phoning? and do you talk to HIM at play rehearsal? Etc.

Two and three times a day we sneaked notes to each other, adorned with hearts and xxxxx's. In them, we tried to top each other with tortured descriptions of what it was like to live in the shadow world of forbidden love—the same sentiments we bleated out

145

to each other in the white Riviera convertible, and walking along chilly, secluded beaches. . . . This can't continue, Henry, Valerie was always telling me: You have to think of something.

We made all the discoveries lovers make about each other: We'd both go to any movie Sean Penn was in (we'd never once been to a movie together), and our favorite songwriter was Michael Jackson, and all TV sitcoms were really boring. . . . Our favorite old rerun was *M*A*S*H*, and we both hated computer games but got hooked on them once we started playing one.

She told me someday she hoped to work in publishing or write a novel. She told me that she loved a writer named Joan Didion. I said so did I, even though I didn't know such a writer. I said I liked J. D. Salinger. She said, Oh, Salinger, in a yawn tone, all the assassins in the world are going around with *Catcher in the Rye* in their back pockets!

We collected tiny little pieces of beach glass we put in an old Wish-Bone salad dressing bottle, and took a dozen rolls of film of each other with Valerie's Kodak. We stopped strangers in the dunes and asked them to take pictures of us together. We wrote our names on rocks with Magic Markers, and carved them into trees with my red Swiss army knife. . . . This can't continue, Henry, Valerie was always telling me: You have to think of something!

"Why do *I* have to think of something?" I'd say.

"Your father is the obstacle!" . . . I never told her that all her father's gibes at me and Peter's (he called our place Schnitzel's on TV) were getting to my brothers. They called Valerie Frau Smackensmarter or Frau Embracenbrighter, and they called him a lot worse. A *lot* worse, while I shouted back that they were Nazis.

"You have to outwit Daddy," Valerie insisted. "Win him over, impress him, do *something* to make him change his mind about you!"

"Like *what*? He won't even let me near the house! I can't even call you!"

"I know it," she always agreed in a hopeless-sounding voice.

Sometimes we talked about running away together, but Valerie talked more about how she prayed she'd be accepted at Antioch. . . . Sometimes we pretended we were years married, with our kids in the backseat of the car coloring, while we promised them ice cream cones as soon as we saw a Carvel stand along the road. We'd named our little boy Hank (Henry Jr.) and our little girl Helene.

We drove around the little beach towns outside Seaville picking out houses we envisioned ourselves raising a family in, and we planned a long honeymoon trip through Europe, deciding the actual wedding would take place in Paris.

"Maybe we'll even exchange our vows in French!" Valerie said.

"French is my worst subject," I said.

"What am I saying right now?" she said. *"Je t'adore."*

"You're saying shut the door," I teased back.

"Henry!"

"Shut the door, shut the door, shut the door!" I said. We began writing that at the end of our notes, and when I'd see Jody in school, I'd tell her to tell her sister shut the door.

Jody'd say, "I'm not carrying coded messages! Give it to me straight or get another go-between."

Worse even than the idea of having to sneak around to see each other was the idea of Valerie going off to some place like Antioch in the fall and our not being able to be together at all.

When Valerie went to have her photograph taken for the Seaville High yearbook, she said, "I refused to smile, Henry. I tried to tell you I love you with my eyes, so every time you look at my picture you'll see me saying that."

My school marks slid, and I lost weight, lost track of how many dinners we did a week, what Earl and my mother were up to, what anyone was up to but Valerie. When Lena made a limp attempt to respond to my valentine with a friendship card showing two elephants shaking trunks, I couldn't even call her face to my mind's eye. When Piddle stood over me in class, and thundered out with dragon eyes that I had better be prepared to deliver my baby with more intelligence than I'd carried it, I was indifferent to his threats . . . and also barely passing his course, he told me.

Mid-April, Valerie heard she'd been accepted at Antioch. I toyed with the idea of dropping out of school and the family business, and following Valerie to Ohio, and getting a job there. Threats and boasts to do this would sink us both into a deep depression. I could see myself working nights in a Taco Bell, while Valerie dated college men on their way to becoming lawyers, architects, and M.B.A.s.

Valerie sometimes said she'd never be happy, even at Antioch, without me, so she'd wait until I was graduated, and we'd go to college together. We'd get married and take turns working to put each other through. She'd add, "All you have to do is decide what you want to be!" and somehow it would seem like another accusation. It would seem like I'd never choose anything but a poo, hardly worth her giving up her family money for, her pink-rose-white-background, soap-in-the-shape-of-a-rose world, dreams of Antioch, and comfort of being Daddy's tweet Valley pussums. This can't continue, Henry, Valerie would whimper, you have to think of something!

The day before *Our Town* was to be performed, Valerie picked me up in front of Nelson Flower's. There was a new, gay glint to her light-green eyes, and the slanted smile kept growing to a broad grin.

"Guess what, Henry! Daddy's flying in from Vegas tomorrow, just to see the play!"

She babbled away before I could think of any response. "He's never seen me act before! It wasn't easy for him to get away, either! He told me on the phone he was just going to do it! 'How often do I get to see my Valley strut her stuff,' he said! Oh, Gawd, I'll probably mess up all my lines! Now the entire family's going to be there, even Vivienne."

"Is she bringing her telephone?" I said in a much too sour voice.

"And my Uncle David and my Aunt Birdie are coming from Bellport! You'd think it was a Broadway opening!"

I'd planned to tell her that the only member of my family who'd arranged to see the play had suddenly canceled out. . . . Angel. . . . Angel had flown the coop, leaving Fred a note saying, "I've had it up to here out here!" She'd left the ticket to the play stapled to the note, and Earl T. Farr had bought it from Fred, in a fit of compassion, even though I insisted I only had three lines, and he'd just make me nervous.

Earl T. Farr'd waved away my protests. "Your mom and Ernie and Fred will hold down the fort at Peter's, and I'll be in the cheering section at your school!"

Valerie said she had to drive me right home because her Uncle David and Aunt Birdie and Vivienne were arriving that afternoon and staying over. "We've got a houseful, Henry, so I have to help out. You understand, don't you?" . . . I was too down to give her any of my news.

"I'm glad he's coming for your sake," I said, "but the thought of him out there in the audience with me doesn't thrill me." I spoke my lines from the audience, and I had sudden visions of a lit cigar at the back of my neck, or hands coming from behind while thumbs pressed hard against my throat.

"Just wow him like I intend to!" Valerie told me.

"How am I going to wow him like you intend to? I have three lines, and I'm not his daughter."

"Just pack everything you have into those three lines, Henry. Just make him see everything I see in you!"

"Please," I said, holding both my hands to my forehead where I was beginning to feel sharp pains.

"Oh, Henry," she wailed, "you have to think of something! Can this continue?"

The following afternoon I did double duty in the kitchen of Peter's, to make up for the fact I'd be missing for three nights from the dining room. I chopped meat, rolled out dough, wrapped sausages, and cut up cabbage.

Ernie kept telling me it was a good thing to be

involved in school activities, getting flour all over the arm of the telephone, and down into the receiver, while he dialed the numbers of likely part-time waiters. Fred was working on a long letter to Angel, while he cut up lemon and lime peels for drinks and refilled the maraschino cherry jar. . . . "I don't want to beg," he told me, "but I don't want to come off like I don't know what she means. . . . Henry? Should I send a card instead? Would it be possible to find a card with an angel on it? A miss-you card with an angel?"

"I don't have time to shop for a miss-you card with an angel on it," I told him.

"I never should have let you send that valentine with the angel on it to Lena," he said.

"You didn't want to give it to Angel," I reminded him.

"Who thought after all this time she was still into angels?" Fred said.

Ernie said, "Once a woman's into something, she's into it, Fred. Let her forget you're not into it anymore, and pfffft!"

So much for Schiller philosophy.

Wafting through the heavy aroma of cabbage cooking and sausage frying, wiggling its way out of the melody of the oompah band tuning up in the dining room, and floating down to hover above my head, until it was transmitted to my brain cells, was an idea. Out of thick air. A plan.

I showered and shaved with a song in my heart,

and dressed with a tiny smile flickering at the corners of my mouth. I sailed into the living room and hugged my mother, who said, "Good luck, darling. I wish I could be there to see you."

"Maybe it's just as well," I told her.

While Earl T. Farr drove me to Seaville High in his new Ford, I hummed to the radio, aware that he was giving me sideways glances.

"I know how it is," he told me. "You get so nervous you get giddy."

But he didn't know how it was.

Only I knew how it was, and what there was that had to be done.

I took the seat reserved for me in the audience, and kept my eyes down, my heart from ripping through my shirt, my head cool.

The auditorium was packed. *Our Town* was sold out.

Wherever Al Kiss was in that audience, I wanted no glimpse of him, no glimmer of Jody's braces flashing in the light to signal where the Kissenwiser brood was staked out. (Did Valerie's mother show? She who never remembered Valerie was to play Emily, or even that she was in a play called *Our Town*?)

Seaville High's principal, Mr. Netzer, was soon onstage holding his hands up for silence, and then beginning his short welcoming speech.

As Act One commenced, with Stage Manager beginning, "This play is called *Our Town*. It was written

by . . ." My armpits were already small fountains.
Soon, Valerie was saying her first line.

EMILY: *I'm both, Mama: you know I am. I'm the brightest girl in school for my age. I have a wonderful memory.*

We were getting closer.

WOMAN IN THE BALCONY [Marilyn Klaich, locker next to mine]: *Is there much drinking in Grover's Corners?*

Closer.

My eyes stayed in the direction of my Weejuns, and my navy socks.

My cue then: . . . *Right good for snake bite, y'know—always was.*

I was on my feet.

TALL MAN AT BACK OF AUDIENCE [me]: *Is there no one in town aware of—*

STAGE MANAGER: *Come forward, will you, where we can all hear you—*

I walked down the aisle.

TALL MAN: *Is there no one in town aware of social injustice and industrial inequality?*

154

MR. WEBB: *Oh, yes, everybody is—some-thin' terrible. Seems like they spend most of their time talking about who's rich and who's poor.*

Tall Man departed from the script.

TALL MAN: Him *she loves? Yes, Mr. Kiss, your daughter loves him. And I, sir, love your daughter.*

Murmuring growing like the sounds of distant thunder, and all eyes were fixed to me.

TALL MAN: *I love Valerie Kissenwiser! I, Henry Schiller, am in love with the daughter of Al Kiss, who* says *he understands love, so he ought to understand what is driving me to this very act! Desperation is driving me. Passion is driving me!*

I could hear Mr. Piccara's voice crying out, "Get that nut!"

I could hear footsteps behind me.

TALL MAN: Him *she loves? Yes! She loves him!*

Hands on my arms.

155

TALL MAN: *He loves her!*

I was being pulled backward.

TALL MAN: *We love each other!*

Commotion was exploding in the auditorium and I was being dragged up the aisle.

TALL MAN: *We love each—*

and an enormous palm was clapped across my mouth.

But I went out to applause.

Yes!

It started with weak, scattered clapping, a whistle, a cheer, and as I was yanked through the doors and into the corridor, I could hear the kind of soaring applause that usually comes as a curtain is dropped.

16

After that night, there was good news and bad news.

There was more bad news, though, than good news.

Our principal, Mr. Netzer, informed me that I was thereafter forbidden to participate in any of Seaville High's extracurricular activities. . . . I was to be off the school property ten minutes after the last bell.

While Ernest Leogrande and Jonathan Karpinski headed down to the field for baseball practice, I headed down the front walk leading away from S.H.S.

While Coach Keene interviewed likely prospects for the fall football team during gym, I did the routine calisthenics with all the ones chosen last for competitive games.

Jody had broken down and confirmed the Kissenwisers' worst suspicions: Valerie and I had been carrying on behind their backs.

Valerie's mother drove her to and from school in a brown Eldorado with a license plate reading K I S S. She was no longer allowed to drive her own car anywhere.

The very first communication I had with her was a note delivered by Nelson Flower that looked like a child's finger painting.

It said, *This is being written in my blood, Henry. There is no other way to tell you how much more I love you!* There was a brownish-colored heart with an arrow going through it under the words.

We purposely bumped into each other in the halls of Seaville High, gasping out loving declarations, never sure which faculty member would be cruel enough to call the Kissenwisers and say, "They're still at it."

Our correspondence rivaled that of legendary lovers separated by oceans and wars, and anyone and everyone was willing to act as courier, eager for a role in our romantic drama.

We were the School Lovers, but whatever glory there was in finding stolen moments by the drinking fountain, in front of bulletin boards, around corners, and behind doors wasn't enough to make up for the fact we were never alone, or locked in steamy embraces, or unwatched.

"Daddy said if it's war your Heinrich wants, he's

got it!" Valerie wrote in one note. "Daddy said you don't even know from big guns yet!"

Al Kiss was threatening to take Valerie and Jody to Europe for the summer.

Al Kiss was talking about renting the house on Ocean Road and moving the family to Martha's Vineyard for the summer.

My grades were sliding way down, and all my teachers were telling me to shape up or ship out. . . . "Eros," Piddle was reminding me once a week, "is fast becoming your nemesis, Mr. Schiller!"

The good news was that business was picking up at Peter's, not just because the weather was warming up and weekenders were pouring into the area. More and more customers wanted to know if we were really Schnitzel's, if I was really Heinrich.

Once, when I knew the Kissenwisers were giving a party in a tent behind their house, to honor Mrs. Trump's eighty-third birthday, I borrowed against my salary to send three bouquets of a dozen Mylar balloons each. Balloon-O-Gift delivered them to the party, with streamers attached reading HENRY LOVES VALERIE.

Once, when *The Seaville Star* printed an interview with Al Kiss, showing a photograph of him with the caption *Al Kiss, Loving Father and Family Man*, I cut it out of the paper. (The whole family was in the background, even Nachus.) I pasted it to a piece of cardboard, and I wrote underneath:

> Q. *What are the three errors in this photo?*
> A. *1. Al Kiss loving.*
>   *2. Al Kiss loving father.*
>   *3. His fangs aren't showing.*

I sent it off to him, special delivery, then lost my appetite for days over the realization it just wasn't that clever. It wasn't big guns. . . . I needed big guns.

I sent a gift-wrapped catnip mouse to Nachus from Loving Pets, with a card reading, "Keep on hissing!" and nearly doubled over in pain after I left the shop, knowing I was still trying to bring down a rhinoceros with darts. . . . I needed big guns.

I took long walks by myself along beaches where Valerie and I had run, trembled, kissed, leaned down to pick up bits of colored glass, and warned Hank and Helene to stay out of the surf.

"He's investigating tennis camps for me!" Valerie wrote in one note. "Camp—at my age! I'd be a laughing stock!"

One afternoon when my mother was trying to get me to eat something, she looked across the table at me and said, "I blame myself, Henry."

"For what?"

"For what you're going through. I should have realized what the business has done to you. No won-

160

der you get caught up in these obsessions! You've never had time to ease into a normal boy-girl relationship. Earl pointed that out to me."

"What does Earl know? That night he drove me home from the play he said he'd never make a fool of himself for any female. He said never lose your composure, Henry, because you'll lose the girl."

"Well? Do you have the girl?"

"She sat down and wrote me a letter in her own blood because I did that. Do you think anyone's ever written Earl T. Farr in her own blood?"

"And where's a letter written in Valerie Kissenwiser's blood going to get you, Henry? Not on the baseball team. Not on the football team. . . . You're letting the best years of your life slip by because of these obsessions, and I blame myself."

"Don't put Valerie in the same category with Kelly and Lena."

"Oh, I don't. Don't worry. She has her own special category, and so does that father of hers!"

"He hasn't hurt business."

"We're not Disneyland where people come to see the sights. We're a restaurant . . . and I think you should let Fred and Ernie and me run the business for a while. I think you should concentrate on school, and friends. I think you should have evenings to yourself. Call up friends, go to movies. You used to like to bowl."

"What will I use for money?"

"Earl says you can work in his used-car lot a few afternoons a week and weekends."

"No," I said. "He's just trying to worm his way into our life."

"He's already wormed his way into mine," my mother said.

"What do you mean he's already wormed his way into yours?"

"I'm very fond of Earl, Henry. I've been very lonely for too long a time."

I wasn't really listening. "I don't even know what I'm going to be!" I complained, hitting my forehead with my palm. "But I'm not going to sell used cars!" I vowed. "What a poo! A car dealer!"

"What's a poo?"

I told her Al Kiss's theory about a poo.

"What the hell does he think *he* is?" she shouted.

She almost never shouted.

I'd never heard her say "hell" before.

We were all beginning to feel the strain.

I definitely needed big guns.

Meanwhile, I aimed another dart at the rhinoceros.

I had a pizza delivered to the Kissenwisers' house on a Friday night I knew he was there. I slipped in a blown-up photograph of Valerie and me hugging each other, on the dunes, to rest on top of the sausage and anchovies.

Across the photograph, in red, I printed:

Q. Which word doesn't belong in this group?
A. Valerie.   B. Henry.   C. Love.
D. Happiness.   E. Daddy.

April dragged on—the cruelest month, someone once said about it. Someone was right.

Daddy says may all your teeth fall out but one, Valerie wrote me.

Why all but one? I wrote back.

So in one you have a permanent toothache, she answered.

I flunked a French test; got a D—with a warning in red—on a Contemporary History paper. I replaced Nelson Flower as Piddle's prize scapegoat. ("He thinks you're coasting, Henry," Nelson told me. "He likes it best when you come up with new information on your condition.")

On a slow Monday evening, Earl T. Farr asked Fred, Ernie, and me to have a drink with him in the bar.

"Boys," he began, "I guess it's no secret to you that Earl's Real Pearl is none other than your beautiful mother. I would like your permission to make her Mrs. Earl T. Farr."

I went to sleep with a blinding headache, and woke up in the middle of the night from a dream that Nachus was walking down my body, her tail tickling my nose.

"ACH-CHOO!" I sneezed. "ACH-CHOO!" and

the sneeze sounded for all the world like the terrible sneeze of Al Kiss.

Then and there those five words came to me: THE SNEEZE OF AL KISS.

And I knew suddenly that I had a big gun.

17

"But what does it mean, Henry?" Valerie asked me when she saw the T-shirt I'd had made for myself (and another for Nelson Flower).

WATCH FOR THE SNEEZE OF
AL KISS

"It doesn't really mean anything," I told her. "That's the beauty of it. Everyone will be waiting to see what it means."

We were squeezed against the blackboard, behind the door of Miss Greenwald's room, Valerie's home-room. Miss Greenwald always stayed in the faculty lounge, smoking, until first bell.

165

"I don't get it," Valerie said. ". . . Oh, Henry, you smell of toothpaste. I can just see you stumbling out of bed, going across your room to your bathroom. I bet you squeeeze the toothpaste tube from the top."

"I go across the hall to the bathroom," I said. "I share the bathroom with two other people. I squeeze the toothpaste tube from the middle. . . . Just get me those names and addresses and phone numbers I want, will you? Do you trust me?"

"Is Paris a city? You'll have them tomorrow. What kind of toothpaste do you use?"

"Crest," I said. We were so close we were almost kissing.

"I use Listerine," she said. "I use Formula 409. I use Shalimar. I use Pantene shampoo. I want you to know everything personal you can know about me."

"I'd rather find out for myself," I told her. She was eating my left earlobe.

"I sleep in the raw," she whispered into my ear.

"I saw a nightie hanging on the back of your bathroom door," I said, rubbing my nose along her cheek.

"I just wear that to walk around in front of windows nights."

"What time?"

"Will you be out in the bushes looking up at my window?"

"Is a Jaguar a car?"

"GOOD MORNING, MISS GREENWALD!" Nelson Flower shouted from the hall.

166

"Don't forget," I told Valerie, "get as many names and addresses as you can."

"What is the sneeze of Al Kiss?" Miss Greenwald was asking Nelson, as I slipped out the door.

"It's just something to watch for, Miss Greenwald."

While I was opening my locker, Marilyn Klaich said, "Hi, lover boy. What's the sneeze of Al Kiss?"

"It could be a rock group," I said.

"Is it?"

"Or a play."

"I thought you two were big enemies."

"It could be a big enemy," I said. "It's something to watch for."

The next morning, Valerie passed me an envelope with the names and addresses and phone numbers of people like Merv Griffin, Joan Rivers, Alan King, Phyllis Diller, Liz Smith—all entertainment people, or newspaper columnists, club owners, publicity people—three sheets of typed information copied from Al Kiss's address book.

Nelson and I spent the afternoon in the Seaville library making up fliers and stuffing them into envelopes.

WATCH FOR THE SNEEZE OF AL KISS

"Can I order anything I want on the menu?" Nelson asked me. "Or do I have to order the special?"

"I told you, Nelson. Anything you want. It'll be on me."

"I'm going to order schnitzel à la Holstein," he said, "and either Bavarian pudding or apple strudel."

"You can have both," I said. "You're a big help."

"I don't like to be called big," he said. "I get that all the time."

"You're a great help, Nelson."

Angel'd been asking Fred to please send all her angels to her, and I told Fred I'd deliver them personally on the Hampton Jitney. I'd take the afternoon jitney into New York and return on the last one that evening.

"Tell her I just mope around," Fred said.

"Why don't you tell her that?"

"I asked her to come back three times. Tell her I just mope around. It's more authentic coming from one of the family."

Angel was watching an old Joan Crawford movie when I got to her mother's apartment on West Twenty-eighth Street.

"You have to help me, Angel," I said. "I really didn't come here just to return your angels. I admit that."

"Are you in trouble, Henry?"

"Something like that," I said, and I explained what I wanted her to do.

168

She just looked at me for a long while.

"It sounds crazy," she finally said. "Most of these people won't even come to the phone, will they? I'll get their secretaries or their answering machines."

"Perfect!" I said. "Try one, Angel, while I'm still here."

She brushed her black hair back from her face, let out a long sigh, and picked up the telephone.

She dialed and waited through the rings.

"You see?" she said. "It's an answering machine."

"Wait for the beep," I said. "Then go ahead."

Angel waited. Then she went ahead. "ACH-CHOO! Watch for the sneeze of Al Kiss. . . . ACH-CHOO! Watch for the sneeze of Al Kiss. . . . ACH-CHOO! Watch for the sneeze of Al Kiss."

After, she looked up at me and giggled. "It's kind of fun, Henry."

"Oh, Angel, you don't know what a great help it'll be to me!"

"You want to know something, Henry?" she said. "This is the very first time anyone in the Schiller family has asked me to help with anything. Maybe what you're asking me to do is something crazy, but at least you're asking for my help. I was never even asked to set a table in the place, or sit at the bar and keep Fred company, or fill in for the coat check girl, never, in all the years I've been married to Fred!"

"He just mopes around, Angel."

"That's his trouble," she said.

"No. I mean, he just mopes around since you've been gone."

"I remember Fred when he was something like you, Henry. But all the zip went out of Fred. Don't let the zip go out of you, Henry."

"I won't," I promised.

I left all the telephone numbers with Angel, and spent the rest of the time taking around fliers to clubs where Al Kiss appeared.

WATCH FOR THE SNEEZE OF AL KISS

I visited Quikprint and had 500 business-size cards made up:

WATCH FOR THE SNEEZE OF
AL KISS

I handed some of them out on Fifth Avenue, Park Avenue, Lexington, and Third, before I caught the jitney back to Seaville.

Nights, I slipped them into the pockets of customers' coats, gave some to Nelson to distribute through the town, and mailed others out to the master list.

Al Kiss was appearing at a club in Atlantic City, and I sent fliers to the club, neighboring clubs, and the hotels and newspaper.

Nelson and I passed out cards to passengers waiting

170

for a day-trip bus to Atlantic City, mostly senior citizens going there to gamble.

"What *is* the sneeze of Al Kiss?" they wanted to know.

"Everyone's asking that," we told them.

"He's gotten wind of it," Valerie wrote me in one of her notes, "but I don't think he suspects you're behind it. People are sneezing at him, Henry! He said on the phone someone sneezed real loud in his audience and everyone laughed."

Nelson and I didn't let up.

"How come Nelson gets full dinners on the house?" Ernie wanted to know.

"He's helping me with a school project," I said.

"Why are you asking for all these advances on your salary?"

"It's part of the same deal, Ernie."

"You can't buy good grades, Henry. You have to earn them."

I changed the subject. The last subject I wanted to discuss was my grades.

On a weekend Al Kiss flew into Seaville from Atlantic City, it got a small notice in the column of a New York newspaper.

ACH-CHOO! Can anyone tell this columnist what the sneeze of Al Kiss is?

Sunday morning, while my mother and Fred and Ernie were at church, Valerie called.

171

"He's seen the fliers, Henry! He knows it's you."

"What did he say?"

"He told one of his stories. You know his stories that have morals?"

"Tell the story."

"I hope I can get it right. It was something about this lion who thought he was so ferocious that he ate a bull. He felt so good about eating the bull, he gave a big roar. . . . I hope I'm getting this right."

"Go on, Valerie. The lion ate the bull and gave a big roar."

"Right. A hunter heard him roar and shot him."

"And?"

"And Daddy said when you're full of bull, you should keep your mouth shut, or you'll end up dead," Valerie said. "I hope I got it right."

"It sounds like you got it right," I said.

"Oh, Henry . . . I don't think this sneeze thing was such a good idea. . . . He's going to be on *Celebrity Quizz* tomorrow. He's filling in for somebody."

"What time?" I said.

"We'll be in school, Henry."

"What time?" I said.

"One o'clock in the afternoon. . . . I'm writing you a long note, Henry. . . . That's what I'm doing over here."

"I'm studying French," I said.

"Shut the door, Henry."

"Shut the door," I said.

172

———————

The next afternoon, my mother watched *Celebrity Quizz* for me.

When I came home from school, I asked her what happened.

"It's just one of those quiz shows," she said. "He won three hundred dollars for someone in Newark because he could name six of the original thirteen states."

"Was there anything about a sneeze?"

"Yes, there was," she said. "What *is* all this about a sneeze?"

"Please just tell me what there was about a sneeze."

"When he came on, the M.C. sneezed."

"And?"

"And Al Kiss said, 'God bless you,' and the M.C. laughed and said, what is there about *your* sneeze, Al? We're all waiting for the answer to that one. And Al Kiss said he was working on the answer."

"That's all?"

My mother shook her shoulders. "That's all. He acted like he didn't want to talk about it. He said he was working on the answer."

I blew the last of my money on telegrams to talk-show hosts and newspaper columnists:

WATCH FOR THE SNEEZE
OF AL KISS

Nelson and I made posters, and talked local store owners into putting them into their windows, telling them they were publicizing a local star's new movie.

"So that's what this is all about!" one said.

Another said, "We keep the cigars he smokes on order. He smokes Schimmelpennincks."

One morning, Valerie and I sneaked a kiss by the water fountain at school, and she said, "Everybody everywhere is sneezing at Daddy, Henry. I'm beginning to feel sorry for him."

"What about feeling sorry for us?"

"I know it," she said sadly, "but poor Daddy. People call the house and sneeze into the phone. Just the other night—"

"Here comes Jody," I said.

We jumped apart.

On the afternoon Al Kiss was to appear for a charity benefit in a town ten miles from Seaville, I was stopped midway through a recitation in French class.

"*Non,* Henry!" Mademoiselle Lane said. "*Contretemps.* Not con-tree-temps. Now say it, Monsieur Henri!"

"Con-tres-temp."

"*Non, non, non.* Listen: kohnh-tre-tahnh."

"Kohnh-tre-tahnh!"

"*Oui!* And what does it mean?"

"It means an embarrassing mishap," I said.

———

Late that night, in the parking lot outside the Oceanview Community House, Nelson Flower told me he was scared.

"Just keep doing it," I said. "We're almost finished."

"My soap is starting to lather from the sweat in my hands," Nelson said.

I passed him a chunk of my own dry Dial.

We'd soaped WATCH FOR THE SNEEZE OF AL KISS across the windshields of Toyotas, Fords, Chevrolets, Mercedeses, Corvettes, Audis, BMW's, Fiats, and Cadillacs.

"I think one of the valets saw us," Nelson whined.

"Nobody's paying any attention to us," I said. "They're all trying to spot celebrities."

"We've done enough," Nelson said. . . . "I'm getting tired of German food, anyway."

"Good!" I said. "Because you're eating us out of business!"

"Let's quit, Henry. Let's try to sneak in and see the show."

"We need tickets," I said, leaning across the front of a Chrysler.

"We could sneak in. I know we could."

"We've only got one more row to go."

"WHAT ARE YOU DOING?"

"Did you say something, Henry?" Nelson asked.

"Was that you, Nelson?" I said.

"WHAT DO YOU CALL THIS?"

And so began a contretemps.

175

18

"Speaking of getting arrested," Al Kiss said to me in the Oceanville Police Station, "when I first met Valley's mother, I couldn't even get arrested. You know that expression? I was zero, poorer than a pauper, with a bigshot mouth on me that wouldn't quit. I was a young *luftmensh*—you know what that means? It's Yiddish from German."

"I don't speak Yiddish or German," I said.

We were sitting on a bench in front of the sergeant's desk.

Nelson Flower's father had already come to get him.

I was waiting for Ernie to get there from Seaville.

"*Luftmensh*," Al Kiss said. "*Luft* means air. *Mensh* is man. It means airman. Not an aviator, though. Someone with his head in the clouds and he's not flying a plane. Some *shlimazel* who's talking I'm going to play this club, be in that show, get an act, soon as my agent, soon as a contract . . . and I'm lucky to be singing 'Oh, My Papa' in some moth-eaten lounge in Philadelphia, where they water the scotch and the star hangs up his coat in the broom closet next to the Men's."

Ernie was going to kill me.

It was a Thursday night, good for seventy dinners minimum. Fred had taken his car into New York to see Angel. I had Peter's Jeep Wagoneer.

How was Ernie even going to get to Oceanville?

"Heinrich, are you listening?"

"My name's Henry," I said.

"Henry . . . I couldn't even get arrested when I was first seeing Miriam. You couldn't tell *me* that, though. Ida Trump knew. Valley's grandmother is an A-1 *shlimazel* spotter. If there was a reward for every *shlimazel* that old lady ever spotted, she'd be richer than God. She's got more IBM stock than He's got, already. . . . She spotted you the day you came to brunch. 'Hoo-ha,' she says, 'there's a *shlimazel* who doesn't know his *ponim* from his *pupik*.' *Ponim* is face, and your *pupik* is your belly button."

Al Kiss had tried to get me off, once he'd heard about the ruckus in the parking lot.

177

But the director of the Oceanview Community House (the same one who gave me a fat lip and the black eye when I made a break for it) had already placed charges. Assault, damaging property . . . and the police had thrown in resisting arrest.

Al Kiss had tried to put up bail, but by the time he got to the police station, Ernie was on his way.

"What's the big *megillah*?" Al Kiss had asked the police officers. "You're thrown in the tank for soaping windows? Is this Russia?"

The police didn't make me wait for my brother in a cell. They let me sit on a bench in front of the desk, with Al Kiss.

He had on a tux, black tie undone, what hair he had mussed, a cigar clutched between his fingers.

"You know who you reminded Ida If-I-Don't-Get-You-in-This-Life-I-Will-in-the-Next Trump of?"

"Who?"

"Alan Kissenwiser. That was me before I circumcised my name."

I didn't say anything.

I was worried about our restaurant license. I was trying to remember something about losing a liquor license if you hired anyone with a police record.

I remembered my mother's tone of voice. "All right, Henry. Wait right there. Ernie will come . . . somehow."

I could see her eyes in my memory, the same expression in them when a police officer told her my father was dead. It's hard to describe. It was like someone socked her in the gut: the punch registered, she stepped back, took it all in, then stepped forward—ready to go on. All that in a flicker. She was good at that expression.

"Do you know what I'm talking, Heinrich?"

"Henry."

"Do you know what I'm saying to you, Henry?"

"No."

I was tired, too . . . beat . . . down. . . . An obsession takes it out of you. You wake up in the middle of the night and your motor's still going: I know what I'll do next. . . . I got one this time. . . . Here's an idea. . . . You never rest.

I was starting to crash. . . . Okay, I'd sell used Fords. I'd go out with Marilyn Klaich. . . . I'd bowl.

It still hadn't dawned on me what was happening right there in the Oceanview Police Station.

"I'm talking us," Al Kiss said. "You? Me?" He leaned forward and looked over his shoulder at me. "You hear me?"

"Yeah."

"We're not oranges and apples. You know?"

"We're not what?"

"We're not that different, Heinrich . . . Henry. . . . I followed Miriam all the way to Venice, Italy, one summer. The old lady took her there to get her away from me. I turned up in St. Mark's Square at teatime. The two of them are sitting there at this little table. Enough pigeons around their feet to drive a cat bananas. You know how a cat's jaws tremble when he sees a bird? Cat'd go off his rocker seeing those pigeons. . . . The band was playing the tune to 'My beer is Rheingold the dry beer'—what the hell is the name of that song? . . . So I go over to where they're sitting. They both think I'm back in Paramus. I bow low from the waist and ask Miriam to dance."

"Did she?" I was beginning to listen.

"We did a waltz, the two of us, in St. Mark's Square, with all the pigeons flapping their wings and the old lady sitting there in front of her teacup. . . . So I know a little on this love subject."

He patted his chest and said, "I got a wallet in here with half a dollar bill in it. I never go anywhere without it. I got half and Valley's mother's got the other half. You know what's written on my half?"

I had the feeling I knew.

" 'No room is too small,' " Al Kiss said. "Miriam's half says, 'when two people are in love.' "

He took a drag on his cigar.

He said, "You kids didn't invent love. . . . It's been around a long time."

I was rubbing my black eye, and he took a look at it.

"You got quite a shiner there, Henry."

"Yeah," I said.

We sat there for a while.

The policeman behind the desk was reading *People* magazine.

"I was on the cover of that once!" Al Kiss called over to him.

The policeman only nodded.

"Last June," Al Kiss said. "Valley framed it."

We sat there some more.

Then he slapped his knee suddenly and yipped.

I thought he was starting to wail. In a way, he was. He kept hitting his knee with his palm. The wail was the beginning of a long war hoot of a crazy laugh.

"EEEEEEEE OW! HEIN-RICH! Where'd you think up that sneeze shtick! . . . Oh, my God!" and he was bent double, laughing.

That was the moment I saw the three of them heading through the door: my mother, Ernie, and Earl T. Farr.

"Oh oh," I said to Al Kiss. "All of Schnitzel's is here."

19

Ernie lent me his new navy-blue soft flannel blazer, with the brass buttons, and his best rep-stripe bow tie. Fred lent me his sterling silver belt buckle with the *S* engraved on it. My mother wrapped cherry strudel with a pink bow, picked a dozen tulips from our garden, and tied a light-blue ribbon around them. Earl T. Farr let me borrow a late-model red Mustang GT.

On a warm Saturday night in May, with the dogwood in bloom and the smell of apple blossoms in the air, I presented myself at the front door of the Kissenwisers' house on Ocean Road.

Mrs. Trump answered the door.

"From The Restaurant! You making a delivery or coming to dinner?"

I gave her the flowers and the strudel and stepped inside.

"You're early, Heinrich!" Al Kiss called out to me as he came across the black-and-white marble floor. "Valley's still dressing. C'mon with me."

He had on a pair of bright-green pants with little yellow tennis rackets on them, and a yellow short-sleeved shirt with the tiny green alligator on the front.

I followed him down the hall, into a book-lined room off the living room.

"This is my den," he said.

The first thing I saw, on the only wall without books, was a full-color portrait of Jody and Valerie, with a small brass light attached to the top, and a cord running down the side. They were years younger, both with long curls, sitting with their hands folded in their laps, wearing hair ribbons and frilly little party dresses.

"You know what the shrinks say about the time to arrive for a dinner invitation?" Al Kiss asked me. "Sit down," he said, not waiting for my answer.

He said, "The shrinks say if you arrive early, you're anxious. If you arrive right on time, you're compulsive. If you arrive late, you didn't really want to come. . . . Ha ha. Don't be anxious, Heinrich."

I'd given up trying to get him to call me Henry.

I sat down on the leather couch in front of the fireplace, where there was a vase of lilacs instead of logs.

Al Kiss stood on the thick beige carpet in front of a leather armchair, with a table beside it, on its top a highball and an ashtray with a burning cigar.

"You don't want a drink?" he said.

"No, thanks."

"This is where I hang out," he said, waving his arms in a half circle. "I love books. I got that from my father." He reached for a small gold frame on the bookshelf, and passed it across to me. I saw a head shot of an old man in glasses, who looked like he knew what happened after death and none of it was good news.

"He looks stern, but he wasn't," Al Kiss said. "He had a smile that could light up a mausoleum. He was a tailor, but he knew more about what was in these books here than you know about scheming, and what you know about scheming isn't chopped liver."

I handed the picture frame back to him.

He looked down at it, smiling. "He'd tell me if you're ignorant, old age is a famine. If you're learned, it's a harvest." He looked up and over at me. "Do you like books, Heinrich?"

"I like them all right."

"That's me when I was your age. I liked them all right, too. What did I know?"

He put the photograph back on the bookshelf.

"Our house was filled with books," he said, "five times as many as I got squeezed into this one room. My father loved books! I was like you. I liked them all right, as long as I didn't have to open them and maybe get smart."

"It's hard to find time to read," I said.

"Well, you'll have a lot of time to read in the future, if you can't find the time to read now. You'll have time to read in the unemployment line."

I gave a weak little laugh.

"I did a lot of reading in the unemployment line. I opened my mail and read it in the unemployment line. You owe fifty-seven dollars to the telephone company, Al. You owe a hundred and fifty dollars to the dentist. You owe the rent, the heat—the unemployment line's a great place for reading your bills."

He went over and flopped down into the leather armchair, and took a sip of his drink. "My father told me to learn and pray. Pray and learn. I stopped going to synagogue when I was fifteen and I dropped out of school the year after. . . . So here I am." He gave a snort. "Well. We have a saying: *Az ikh vel zayn vi er, ver vet zayn vi ikh.* If I should be someone else, who would be me? . . . But I wish I'd listened to my father. I wish I'd known then what he knew about now, because an ignoramus dances through life wearing lead shoes. . . . So how are you tonight, Heinrich?"

"Well," I started, but I didn't need a finish.

185

Al Kiss said, "You know I always wanted a son? I always thought of myself sitting in some room like this one talking to my boy. I wanted a boy who'd make a Bar Mitzvah, a kid I'd pass on all my father said to me, half of which I heard. . . . Do you remember your father well?"

"I remember him."

"Well?"

"Do you mean what he said, things he said?" I didn't feel like suddenly snapping my fingers in the air and crying out, "Wait a min-ute! I just thought of something! My father said a turtle never gets anywhere unless he sticks his neck out!" . . . I didn't want to bowl him over with that much originality so early in the evening.

"I mean, do you remember things he told you, things he believed in?"

How about add a little vinegar to the cooking water, to keep the cabbage green and the beets red?

"I don't remember a lot of that," I answered.

"Do you go to the cemetery?"

"It's in Brooklyn."

"So? My father's grave is in Paramus, over in New Jersey? I go there a couple of times a year. Not to keep up the grave, but to keep him up on things. That's where I talk to him. That's part of the continuity."

"I don't do that," I admitted.

"When we say Kaddish—that's our prayer for the dead—we don't say anything about death in it. It's a prayer about continuity. The name of the departed is bound up with the ancestors, and the unborn. . . . I like all that. *Now.* When I was your age, I didn't know what they were talking: tradition, ceremony, customs, community. I was a feather that didn't know I was on a bird. I thought I was flying all by myself."

I could hear Valerie's voice calling from a distance. "Daddy? Henry?"

Al Kiss picked up something next to his highball. He passed it across to me.

It was a crystal paperweight. Inside there was a dirty piece of yellow cloth, in the shape of a star.

"I had that put in there," he said. "You know what that is?"

"It looks like a Star of David."

"My grandmother wore that on her coat sleeve in Belgium. Jews were required to wear one of those under Hitler. Her whole family was taken away— husband, mother, father, sisters. A Belgian family saved her, hid her."

"Daddy?" Valerie's voice. "Henry?"

"We're in here, honey!" Al Kiss called out. ". . . My father used to tell me God is everywhere. Oh yeah, I'd tell him. Where was He when there were concentration camps? 'God is where man lets Him in,' he'd answer; 'Man didn't let Him into concentration

187

camps.' . . . You can say that again! Since concentration camps I know I'm on a bird. I'm not a feather flying all by myself."

Valerie came into the den looking more beautiful than I'd ever seen her, all in yellow, even yellow pumps, and a yellow hairband, with loopy gold earrings on and a big smile.

She actually kissed me on the lips, right in front of him.

"Oh, Daddy!" she said. "Did you have to get out the paperweight?"

"The paperweight was out. It's always out."

"Did you have to call attention to it? That's so gross!"

"I was making a point to Heinrich here."

"Henry," Valerie said.

"Or Sauerkraut Breath," I said.

Al Kiss looked across at me and laughed. I laughed, too.

"That's right, let's try for a little levity," said Valerie. "This is *supposed* to be a fun evening."

The fun evening got under way in the dining room, under the crystal chandelier, shortly after the arrival of Ronald Feldman, Jody's date.

I hadn't seen him since he was John Lennon at the Dead of Winter Dance, wandering around the gym in lensless eyeglasses singing "Imagine."

He was taller and thinner than his older brother,

dressed in chinos and a white shirt, with a light-blue cashmere sweater which he kept knotted around his neck all through dinner. His eyes were a matching blue shade, and he didn't look like he needed to shave yet.

He was proof that Ida Trump could smile. She sat beside him, beaming up at him, making sure he was passed salt, pepper, second helpings of chicken, asparagus, and salad. She called him "Sonny." That's what he looked like, too, this apple-cheeked, peach-fuzz-complexioned kid I imagined putting away his video games to come to dinner.

I sat between Mrs. Kissenwiser, who no one would ever describe as a big talker, and Jody, in pink Calvin Klein jeans and a pink cotton turtleneck sweater.

Valerie sat at one head of the table, her father at the other.

"Sonny" began the conversation by announcing that his brother Trevor was going to M.I.T., but he was aiming for an M.B.A. at H.B.S. (The Feldman boys didn't go to colleges, they went to initials.)

Thus began a spirited, whirlwind exchange between Al Kiss and "Sonny" that lasted through the main course, and was still going on when the maid served the fruit and the white-frosted coconut cake.

It went something like this. "Why H.B.S., Ronald? I know it's good, but there's Wharton, there's Columbia, and Harvard's not that easy to get into, is it?"

189

"I'll get in. I want H.B.S. because I'd rather learn how Ray Kroc founded McDonald's than study the theory of N-Dimensional Security Market Hyperplanes, which is what you study other places."

"You don't like the textbook approach?"

"I don't like it at all. With an M.B.A. from H.B.S., I can start at around thirty-eight thousand. . . . If I go to Wharton, I'd only get about thirty-one; Columbia: the same. The answer to why I want an M.B.A. from H.B.S. is the same one Willie Sutton gave a reporter when he was asked why he robbed banks."

"Because that's where the money is," Al Kiss said.

"Because that's where the money is."

"You want to get into corporate P.R.?" Al Kiss asked him. He said to the table, "Ronald's father's the best P.R. man in the business."

"I'm more interested in R. and D.," said Ronald. "I like research. I like product development. . . . You know why they compare R. and D. to elephants making love?"

"Ha. Ha. Why?"

"There's a lot of trumpeting and writhing in the beginning, but nothing comes of it for at least twenty-seven months."

"Ho! Ho! Ho! I heard it another way. The Mushroom Theory. You stick a bunch of guys in a dark room, dump a pile of manure on them, and see what grows!"

"Hee! Hee! Hee! That's neat, Mr. Kiss. Of course,

a key success factor for any corporate situation is . . ."

Etc., etc.

I was the proverbial bump on the log, the one whose tongue the cat had gotten.

Was it sympathy that moved "Sonny" to direct some conversation toward me, after the coconut cake was served, or some clever instinct motivated by malice?

"What are *you* going to be, Schiller?"

"I haven't really decided yet."

"I may keep him," Valerie spoke up. "He can cook and he's very sexy."

But that little rescue attempt went over like a lead balloon. No one even smiled. Mrs. Trump muttered "sexy" under her breath, with an expression on her face like someone smelling rotten eggs.

"Heinrich's already got himself a business," Al Kiss said. "How come Schnitzel's doesn't need you tonight?"

"Because," I said, wishing I could leave it at that, but plodding on toward further humiliation, "I'm working for Farr Motors now."

"Not for Earl T. Farr?" Ronald Feldman said.

"Who's Earl T. Farr?" Al Kiss asked, forgetting their brief introduction at the Oceanview Police Station.

"He's this nut that climbs out of an oyster shell on television," said Ronald. "You've seen him, haven't you? For a pearl of a car, try Earl T. Farr!"

"Hoo-ha," Mrs. Trump said.

Mrs. Kissenwiser said, "Why don't we all go in the next room so Annabelle can clear the table?"

The evening dragged on, and I felt its weight moving over me like a great wet, thick fog off the ocean. If Valerie felt the same way, she wasn't showing it. Every chance she got she watched me, touched me, smiled at me, and made the words "Let's go!" with her mouth.

I don't know why I didn't take her up on it. I think I kept trying to do something or say something to improve on my poor, poo, mute impression. The lower I sank, the higher Ronald Feldman rose.

He expounded on every subject from software to the Soviet influence in Syria, all the while playing backgammon with Jody on the coffee table in the living room. He advised Mrs. Trump on how to trap the moles invading her vegetable garden, picked up on the fact Mrs. Kissenwiser was exhausted and would just as soon excuse herself and go up to bed, and even told a joke that Al Kiss hadn't heard and that he wrote down in a little leather notebook.

It was Ronald Feldman's evening, hands down.

At one point, I came out of the bathroom downstairs and overheard him as he was discussing me with Al Kiss.

". . . what Val sees in him. He's such a *goyisher kop*."

(I knew what a *goy* was; but what was a *goyisher kop*?)

I saw Al Kiss tap his head with his finger. "He's got it up here. Don't let him fool you. I'm sneezed at in the streets."

I was really moved. He was actually defending me.

Near midnight, Valerie and I finally broke away, after she promised Al Kiss we were only going to go out to the car to talk.

Jody and The Hit of the Dinner Party were still playing backgammon.

Mrs. Kissenwiser was probably fast asleep.

Al Kiss walked us to the door.

"Just a minute," I said. "I'd like to say good-bye to Mrs. Trump."

"Who wouldn't?" he said.

Once we were out in the driveway, in the car, Valerie grabbed me.

"Oh, Henry, I love the way you look tonight. You look so sexy I could eat you up, and I had everything I could do to keep my hands off you!"

"I love you," I said. "I'm crazy out of my head in love with you."

"I can't believe Daddy's come around! And *you* did it!" She was kissing me up and down my neck.

"I actually heard him sticking up for me," I said. "Ronald Success called me a *goyisher kop* and he stuck up for me!"

"Tomorrow let's go someplace very very private and do things," she said, pulling my bow tie loose. "Do you like me to undress you?"

"What's a *goyisher kop* anyway?" I asked her.

She was undoing the top button of my shirt. "It means Gentile brains," she said.

"What's wrong with Gentile brains?"

"They're fine with me," she said.

"You mean just because I don't know what I want to be I'm a *goyisher kop*?"

"Don't worry, Henry. I *will* keep you. Do you eat much?"

"That's not funny," I said. "It wasn't funny when you first said it, either."

"Well, then you have to decide what you want to be," she said. She licked my Adam's apple. "If you can't decide, I'll just have to buy you some white silk pajamas from Dior, and chain you to the bedpost while I go out and earn our living."

"Val-er-rie, that *isn't* funny!"

"Oh, don't be so sensitive," she complained.

But I was suddenly.

Very.

20

"Are you a baseball player, Heinrich?" Al Kiss asked me.

"Yes," I said, eager to impress him finally with something I knew about: sports. "Baseball. Football. Basketball. Some soccer."

"That's your problem. Don't grip or swing the club like it's a bat. You have to master the grip."

Early that Sunday morning, he'd pulled up at Peter's in the brown Eldorado with the KISS license plates. Valerie was still asleep, he said. So was my family. So was most of Seaville. He told me he was taking me for a game of golf. Although I protested I'd never even held a golf club in my hand, we were

195

at the Seaville Golf and Tennis Club half an hour later.

"Team sports are okay for kids," he told me, "but when you get out in the world, you'll want to know golf. It's not only a great game, it's an entree into the business world—*any* business. . . . Keep your left arm straight, Heinrich, my boy!"

In between golf lessons, he expounded on everything from the problem of being outshined by "a twerp like Ronald Feldman," to the problem of raising daughters.

"Do you know how many times I sat there dumbstruck like you sat there last night?" he said. "You want to know what dumbstruck is, walk in a dinner party some time where the other guests are doctors, lawyers, scientists, and you're the show monkey. What do you do, Mr. Kiss? Me? I'm a performer. Where do you perform? Then you got to name all the toilets you worked in in Las Vegas, Atlantic City, and you're talking to people who work in the Pentagon, or at Sloan-Kettering hospital or the Rand Corporation. You feel like a *graubyon*. Someone who's coarse, crude."

"But you're famous, anyway."

"Some famous. . . . Not at those dinner parties. You're the monkey wearing a tie. You're the one who can't come up with anything to say when they're talking M.B.A. at H.B.S."

"You weren't at a loss for words last night."

"I'm talking about you now. Keep your left arm straight, Heinrich. Thatta boy! . . . I can handle a twerp with his sweater around his neck spouting off all through dinner. He's no problem. I don't have to watch his kind, either. His kind wants a hot game of backgammon after dinner. His kind doesn't have my little girl out in the driveway in his car for hours while I sweat."

"We were just talking."

"I know how you two just talk, Heinrich. You two just talk and I just eat my knuckles, because I don't want my little Valley jaded before she even gets to Antioch. Now, jaded's a polite word for what I don't want Valley to be before she even begins freshman year college."

"Yes, sir," I said. What else was I to say? Was I to say his little Valley was the one whose hands reached out first every time we were anywhere alone? Was I to ask him what defense anyone human had against his beautiful, long-soft-black-haired, belt-pulling, heart-ripping Valley?

"We've got a saying," he said. "Many daughters, many troubles. Many sons, many honors. . . . That saying drives Valley up the wall. She says females aren't chattel anymore, and all the rest of that libber crap. She says times have really changed, but do you want to know something?"

"They haven't?" I said.

"They haven't. Valley's mother and I thought Ida

Trump was some relic from the Dark Ages, she was so strict, and now we sit around saying the same things the old lady used to say: She's going to get into trouble if she takes the car. That boy is a boy with his eye on *now*, not a year from now. They're moving too fast. They're too young. Luv-schmuv, they're asking for trouble. . . . We're learning the truth of many daughters, many troubles, and Valley's going to learn it, too. And not too soon, I hope!" He shot me a meaningful look.

"We're not making any plans," I said.

"Maybe that's worse," he said.

I had a sudden vision of Valerie years and years from then, unable to remember her daughter had the lead in a play, sitting through a dinner party silently, all the old zip gone the way Angel said it'd gone out of Fred. Would having daughters do that to her?

I said, "Well, things worked out for you and Mrs. Kissenwiser, didn't they? For all Mrs. Trump's worries, things did work out." I was fishing, to see if he'd agree things had worked out.

"Always hit the ball *hard*, Heinrich," he said. ". . . Yeah, things worked out. Mostly thanks to the old lady. After I got through gambling away every nickel I ever made, she bailed us out. . . . You want to know why I gambled, Heinrich?"

"Because you were working in places like Las Vegas and Atlantic City?"

198

"Partly that," he said. "But more than that, I got into gambling because I didn't have an education. I thought I could earn what those doctors and lawyers earned a year, overnight at the crap table. I was looking for easy money. When you're a monkey in front of a microphone and you're up against the Ronald Feldmans of the world, you look for fast money. . . . What the hell was that twerp wearing his sweater around his neck all through dinner for?"

"I don't know," I said.

"Is that some new style? Maybe he's got a growth coming out of his shoulder blades."

On the way back, Al Kiss said ninety percent of golf was played from the shoulder up. "Ninety percent of life is played the same way," he said. ". . . Do you like golf, Heinrich?"

"I think so, if I can ever get good at it."

"You can," he said. "We'll work on it."

On a Monday morning in mid-May, Piddle banged me across the back of my head with his ruler, and demanded to know what plans I'd made for the home delivery of my child.

"I've changed my mind, sir."

"On your feet, Mr. Schiller!"

I stood up. "I've decided against having my baby at home."

"Explain yourself, Mr. Schiller."

"Well, sir," I began, "I think my baby's health and safety should be the top consideration. I don't want to take the risk of anything happening."

"Like *what*, Mr. Schiller?" He was standing there with his big belly sticking out, mean little eyes fixed on me, ruler ready in his right hand.

"Well, sir, for example, if my baby was born with the umbilical cord twisted around its neck, a pediatrician would be there to give the baby special care, and if the baby needed oxygen—"

I'd done my homework. I had it all down pat.

Piddle gave me grudging praise and went on to bully Nelson Flower.

After class, I returned *Your Baby, Your Body: Fitness During Pregnancy* to him.

"If I have a boy," I said, "I may name him Nelson."

"I think he's going to flunk me," Nelson complained. "You've got an easy problem. There's a beginning and a middle and an end to yours, but mine's just this crappy eating disorder."

"There must be complications involved you're not mentioning," I said. "Piddle thinks you're coasting. You have to come up with something new."

"I'm not going to get into laxatives," Nelson said. "Anorexics take laxatives. Do you think I want to get into that in class?"

"What about the stuff I had to get into?"

"It's not as embarrassing to be pregnant as it is to

be taking laxatives," Nelson said. "And *I* was the one who told *you* Piddle hates coasting. When did you do a turnaround?"

"I want your baby to be a girl," Valerie told me one night when we were studying together at her house.

"Your father says a daughter is trouble, but a son is honor."

"Did he lay that one on you, too?" She was drawing hearts down the side of my French notes. Valerie's way of studying was to open her textbook, then fool around with whatever was in front of me, and my fingers, and the hair at the back of my neck, her long nails trailing down my skin until I got goose bumps and grabbed her.

I'd tell her that I couldn't figure out how she got all A's when she never looked at a book, and she'd tell me she was just naturally brilliant.

"But I'm not. This studying together is the road to ruin for me."

"Playing golf with Daddy is the road to ruin for you," she said. "You're turning into a big bore who brings his books along on dates and isn't even turned on anymore."

"Valerie," I said, "I don't want to be in summer school while you're out sailing and swimming and shopping for clothes to take to Antioch."

"I always feel like Daddy's along on our dates, lately."

She wasn't far wrong. It was hard to do stuff in the backseat of a car with a girl whose father was always telling you he didn't want his little girl jaded before she even got to college.

We were sitting on the floor, in a big pile of pillows, leaning against the couch in the Kissenwisers' living room.

We were waiting for Al Kiss to come on TV, keeping the sound down on *Evening of Stars* until he got onstage.

"Don't pretend you don't know what I'm talking about," Valerie said. "Daddy's been working on you during those golf games, Henry, and it shows."

I made a half-hearted lunge for her, and we wrestled around in the pillows for a while, giggling and tickling each other, but a part of me was detached. A part of me was viewing us from a distance, and remembering other times when being all tangled around her wasn't such a laughing matter.

"There he is!" Valerie said, and she grabbed the remote control and made the sound come up.

"ACH-CHOO!" someone from the audience called out.

Al Kiss began his spiel: "God bless you! Well, Heinrich thinks my sneeze is peculiar, let me tell you about his golf. . . . I play a little golf with him, so I know where he is, and he's not with her. . . . Tee the ball, I tell him. Tee the ball. He says, I *see* it. . . . That's for starters. If he was going to knock my block off, he wouldn't know what club to use. . . . I want to tell you about this Heinrich on a golf course. . . ."

Etc., etc.

I had to laugh. I didn't know why he'd bothered to make up jokes about the way I played golf. The truth was funny enough. We were a comic pair out on the greens. He'd be spouting off words of wisdom, and he'd see what I was doing and he'd shout KEEP YOUR WEIGHT ON YOUR LEFT FOOT! . . . As I was saying, Heinrich, in this life a man is always YOU'RE OVERSWINGING! On and on.

His favorite golf pants were bright red, and his face would turn the same color he'd get so frustrated trying to teach me. . . . A Palmer, a Middlecoff, a Snead you're not! he'd tell me. . . . A wizard with the putter you're not!

A few times he tried out new jokes on me. Once, when I didn't laugh, he said I reminded him of an audience he'd played to in York, Pennsylvania. He said it was like playing to an oil painting: fifty silent faces.

I told him I liked most of his jokes, but jokes about boobs and behinds didn't thrill me. Maybe you've seen too many, he said. In my day there were still some secrets. What secrets does your generation have, hah, Heinrich? . . . Of course, if you don't get an education, you'll keep your salary a secret.

"Oh ha ha ha ha ha!" Valerie said flatly as she watched me crack up at his jokes. "I think you've got a little crush on Daddy."

"ACH-CHOO!" the audience was sneezing at the end of his act instead of applauding. "ACH-CHOO!"

"Hear that, honey?" I said. "They're all sneezing!"

"Maybe he'll ask you to join his act!"

She was putting all the pillows back on the couch where they belonged, throwing them there—hard.

21

It happened on an ordinary day at the end of that very extraordinary May.

May was the month my mother became Mrs. Earl T. Farr, and I became a fairly good beginning golfer, thanks to Al Kiss.

May was the month Angel decided to divorce my brother Fred, and my brother Ernie fell in love with a redheaded widow, who took a job as cashier at Peter's.

And May, filled with heartbreaking, lovely, warm, sunny blue-sky days, was the month Valerie Kissenwiser became more of what she was: more beautiful, sexier, and third in her class, scholastically.

The day I'll never forget began with me picking up the cigars I'd ordered from Tobacco 'N' Stuff. I'd decided to have twins. They'd made up two dozen cigars for me with pink and blue bands, and "Hank and Helene" printed on the cellophane wrappings.

Proudly, I passed them out in Piddle's class, keeping a pair for Valerie and me.

After I explained that my twins were being adopted by a family I'd located through BirthRite ("A wise decision, Mr. Schiller," from Piddle), and after I sat through Nelson Flower's stumbling description of his heavy use of laxatives ("Just part of the nightmare of anorexia nervosa, Mr. Flower, and it's about time you got around to it!"), I raced into the hall at the ringing of the bell.

I was on my way to meet Valerie for lunch.

The twins were to be a surprise. At the same time I'd thought of ordering the cigars, I'd ordered her graduation gift: a silver *chai* pendant, with our initials engraved on the back. I planned to give it to her on prom night. *Chai* meant "life" in Hebrew, and I was working on what I'd write across the gift card. *We'll never say good-bye, just* chai! . . . *To you I'll never lie, or say good-bye, just* chai! (Ernie'd suggested: *You are my high, my* chai!)

When I saw Valerie waiting for me in front of my locker, I hid the cigars in the back pocket of my khakis, and rushed toward her with a big smile.

206

She was frowning, running her finger under the thin gold chain around her neck, tapping her right foot impatiently. Lately, she'd been flaring up over little things. Final exams, I thought, all the frenzy attached to graduation, and the big question mark that was our future were getting to her.

"Where have you *been*, Henry?"

"I just came from Piddle's class. Norman finally—"

She didn't let me finish. "I don't have time for explanations, Henry. I have to meet Marty Wax ten minutes ago to buy the gym decorations for the prom. We can't go out for lunch today."

Noons we'd been driving to McDonald's for Big Macs and Cokes, eating them in her car with the top down, and the tapes playing, fooling around in the sun after, kissing and laughing at the things other kids called out to us. *Him* she loves? was at the top of the list. I admitted to myself how much I liked all that, the public part of it as well as the private part.

"Why did you pick lunch hour to buy the decorations? We always—"

She wasn't in the mood to let me finish sentences. "I didn't pick the time. Marty did. He's chairperson of the prom committee."

"Why didn't you tell him we always—"

"I didn't feel like telling him we always, okay?"

I looked at her, not too taken back by the cool tone, but a little hurt. I felt she took things out on me more and more. Maybe it was my imagination. Maybe it was both of us trying to deal with September coming.

"I have to tell you something else," she said.

I had a feeling I didn't want to hear it, so I didn't ask what the something else was. She'd called me a few unprintable names last Sunday, just because I was a half hour late getting to her house . . . even though I'd phoned her from the club to tell her the golf course was crowded, I was sorry.

"Did you hear what I just said?" she asked me.

"I'm not deaf."

"I don't know any nice way to tell you this, Henry."

The hall was filling up with kids, and there was the sound of shouting, lockers being banged shut, whistling, and there was the darkening shade of her light-green eyes.

My heart went faster.

"Henry," she tried to begin.

I said, "What are you going to tell me in the hall like this? Can't it wait?"

"Marty's asked me to the prom and I've accepted." She said it so fast I wanted to believe I hadn't heard right. . . . Marty?

Marty Wax had played George to her Emily in *Our Town*.

In *Our Town* George and Emily had married each other.

208

"Marty Wax?" I said. The name hung in the air between us like some strange mushroom that appears overnight on your lawn after a hard rain.

I wished I could kick it out of the way with my toe, knock the head off it, but there it was. There he was suddenly in my mind's eye: a senior, president of the Drama Club, owner of a little white Volkswagen convertible, the sort who drove around with the top down on mild winter days. Straight blond hair, always in school plays, his name printed across programs *Martin O. Wax*, a teenage pipe smoker! That alone made him a phony where I was concerned.

"*We're* going to the prom together, Valerie," I said.

"You never asked me."

"What are you talking?" I said. We were going together. We had a six-month anniversary coming up.

"You even sound like Daddy," she said. "Take Daddy to the prom. You two are a perfect couple."

"You were the one who told me to win him over, Valerie."

"Daddy likes to dance. Send him a corsage of roses. He likes red ones. . . . I have to go, Henry. Marty's waiting."

"What are you doing to us, Valerie?"

"You're the one who did it, Henry. I happen to hate boys who feature Daddy over me. All my life I've had to watch out for that!"

209

"You were the one who told me to win him over, Valerie!"

"Stop saying I was the one who told you to win him over! I didn't tell you to turn into his groupie! I'm tired of hearing about you from him, and about him from you! I'm tired of your golf games together, and you cracking up over his jokes, and I'm tired of him being in the backseat of the car with us!"

"Pull-lease!" I said. "Lower your voice."

Kids passing by were slowing up to stare at us.

She lowered her voice. What she said next was hissed out between her teeth. "Since Daddy went to work on you, you've become a lousy lover, too, Henry Schiller! I'm just Daddy's little girl you don't dare do things to!"

"Val-ley!" I gasped. I'd never called her that before. I didn't even know where that came from. It just jumped out of my mouth, unbidden.

"*That* did it, Henry!"

"Val-er-rie," I began, pronouncing all three syllables distinctly, but another voice was interrupting, calling out a newer version of her name. "Valkie?"

"I'm coming, Marty!"

Valkie?

"Valerie," I started over, "I—" but Valerie Kissenwiser wasn't interested in starting over.

She left me there with a nominative singular pronoun dangling, and I watched through a stinging blur of tears, while she walked toward Martin O. Wax.

210

That summer around Seaville, I caught glimpses of her, not many because we weren't very often in the same places.

I spent some time in summer school, repeating the French course I'd flunked. I went shopping for furniture with my brothers, and helped my mother move from Peter's into the new house Earl T. Farr had bought them.

I gave up my job at Farr Motors because business at Peter's was booming, and they needed me.

Part of the reason for the boom was Al Kiss's habit of dropping in, and doing his shtick over our mike, in front of the oompah band.

"*Him* she loves?" he'd always end it, pointing at me, and I'd take a bow, while everyone clapped . . . or sneezed.

Al Kiss wouldn't even let Peter's pick up his bar tab.

"Anything for a friend," he'd say, grabbing my neck in an armlock, grazing my chin with a mock punch.

During our golf games I confessed that I'd begun to take an interest in the restaurant business. I'd already saved enough to put a down payment on the red Mustang, and when we came off the course I had enough money in my pocket to sometimes treat Al Kiss to lunch, instead of always being his guest. I'd bought myself a new blazer like the one I'd always borrowed from Ernie, and I had a little savings account started in the Seaville Bank. . . . A business that paid off that way couldn't be all bad.

But it was more than that. I was becoming a pretty good cook. I'd learned to make soups customers swooned over, and I'd added some American dishes to our menu like corned beef and cabbage and Southern fried chicken. For the first time in my life, I got to know adults who weren't just the parents of some girl I was chasing after, and people over eighteen were asking me how I was.

"It's a good business, isn't it?" I asked Al Kiss. "It's not a poo, is it?"

"Not if you really learn it," he said. "Cornell University gives degrees in restaurant management. Did you know that?"

"I might not even need college."

"Heinrich, a fool takes two steps where a wise man takes none. . . . Up in Ithaca, where Cornell is, there're some beautiful golf courses. They all look out on lakes. There's a lake over every hill up there."

"Maybe I do need college."

"Some maybe. Maybe lungs need air."

We talked about where he was going next with his act. He said Jody'd brought home some kid she met at computer camp named Angus MacGillis. He's the real article, he said, plays bagpipes and begins sentences "I hae na doot" (that's "I have no doubt"). He's over here from Glasgow. . . . Scottish jokes, Al

Kiss said, never offend anyone because the only thing Scots are known for is being thrifty.

"You know the type joke," he said. "A Scot goes into a shop and buys a briefcase. The clerk asks him if he wants it wrapped. He says oh, no, thank you, just put the paper and string inside."

I just looked at him.

"What am I doing, playing to an oil painting again?"

"It's not that funny."

"I've got to work at it. You don't think a good shtick just happens overnight? But it's time to trade you in, Heinrich, for Angus."

We never discussed Valerie, or Marty Wax.

But I saw them sometimes in fleeting glimpses from cars, or ahead of me on streets I walked down. In one fast glimpse I saw Valerie with her arm around him, her finger tucked in the belt loop of his jeans. Another glimpse was of them a few rows ahead of me in the movies, Valerie's head nestling suddenly on his shoulder. One time I saw them at a summer fair, licking ice cream from the same cone.

Each time I felt a long, wrenching pain. My mind ran all the splendid old movies of us hiding inside our coats from the wind and sand in the dunes, in the thrilling days of our forbidden love, of us lighting candles in the car, of us whispering against the walls of schoolrooms, kissing in hallways, fumbling with each other's buttons in the dark, and sitting in the

213

sun outside McDonald's, with music playing and kids watching us.

One very bright, late, Sunday moonlit night, I found myself walking down Ocean Road. I stood outside the Kissenwisers' big white wooden house. There was a light on up in her bedroom. Nachus was sitting in front of the screen in the open window. In another minute, Valerie might have passed by, maybe even wearing the nightie I'd seen hanging from the hook on the back of her bathroom door. . . . I didn't know, but I didn't wait to see, even though I'd probably gone all the way there just to catch another look at her.

I couldn't bring myself to watch her from the bushes. I went instead down to the ocean, and watched the moonlight on the dark water, until the sight of young lovers in the dunes got to me.

Sometimes I looked at the yearbook with her picture, remembering that she said she was telling me she loved me, with her eyes, when the photograph was taken. Sometimes I stared at my half of the dollar bill, or reread the letter she'd written me in her own blood.

Somehow summer passed.

She went on to Antioch College, while I stayed in Seaville.

I kept the cigars with the babies' names on the cellophane, and the *chai* pendant engraved with our

214

initials. She never knew anything about them.

"Always remember," Al Kiss would tell me as we played golf together in the autumn months, "it's today's game that's important. Not yesterday's."

But for a long time, a day didn't pass that I didn't think of her.

About the Author

M. E. KERR was born in Auburn, New York, attended the University of Missouri, and now lives in East Hampton, New York.

In addition to her many novels for young adults, M. E. Kerr has also written ME ME ME ME ME, in which she reveals her own real-life escapades—from first kiss to first publication—and recalls many of the personalities from her life that later emerged as characters in her books.